Experts in martial arts, weapons, and world history, they are Agents of Time. They travel in time in order to track down and kill vampires, werewolves, and those who might fool around with the space-time continuum.

Lorenzo is from Italy. Marie hails from San Diego. Both are as completely different as two people can be, but they have one thing in common—both have had a close encounter with a vampire named Tasia, and lived to tell about it. And it's their destiny to track her down and kill her.

This novel contains danger, menace, elements of horror, paranormal, and time travel.

Date with Destiny
Copyright © 2020 Jon Bradbury
ISBN: 978-1-4874-2933-1
Cover art by Martine Jardin

Published by eXtasy Books Inc or
Devine Destinies, an imprint of eXtasy Books Inc

Look for us online at:
www.eXtasybooks.com or www.devinedestinies.com

DATE WITH DESTINY
ENDS OF TIME BOOK 1

BY

JON BRADBURY

DEDICATION

To Ripley Archer, my Facebook friend who started this book with a writing prompt.

Prologue: This Old House

From the Contact Report of Agent Lorenzo.

Mist began to swirl around my legs as I stepped onto thick, overgrown grass. Thanks to the mist, I nearly bumped into the gate, set in a wall made of brick. The gate itself was made of wrought iron, closed with a heavy iron bar. Beyond the gate, a path laid with stones and bordered with a stone railing disappeared into the mist.

Then I saw the house — more like a mansion or manor — clearly abandoned. It was two stories tall in some sections, with ivy climbing up the walls.

A thoroughly creepy, old, abandoned house. And I had to go in.

She was here. I could feel her presence. I could feel the reverberations of her psyche like ripples in a pond when a raindrop hits the water. Or when a deer feels the wolf's presence.

I should have shifted, but for the time being I needed to remain in human form.

I had hunted Tasia across the ends of time. I had her cornered, with nowhere to run, but at this moment I hesitated, resting my hand on the old wrought iron gate. The reasons for my hesitation were real, and valid.

Tasia was a spirit of darkness and evil. Night was when she was the most powerful. As a spirit of evil, while not all of her powers were explicitly meant for hunting, stalking, and killing, they could still be used for distraction, and were just as bad.

Behind me, the sun was setting, about to dip below the horizon like a molten coin and bring with it the darkness of night.

Ahead of me, the moon was just starting to rise over the horizon, like a bright silver coin of its own. With a jolt of terror, I realized it was a *full* moon. If I wasn't careful, I would have to defend myself against other dangers besides those that fed on human blood.

Where there was a vampire, there was always a werewolf. They tended to operate in pairs, more dangerous together than separately, if they weren't at each other's throats. *Ahem.* Cough. Sorry, bad joke.

The night was already quiet. Usually the crickets were singing their song. But not even the crickets were chirping. Only the whisper of the breeze disturbed my contemplation of this apparently simple gate.

I was feeling confident. Not foolishly so. I had various weapons with me. Some I wore on my person in the form of short swords. Others I carried in a knapsack, the strap of which I had slung over my shoulder. Still others could be employed through hands or mind.

I knew how to use all of them without thinking consciously.

However, I hesitated. And while I had some reasons, I didn't know *why*.

Regardless of the reason, my target was close at hand, and she wouldn't kill herself, unless it was to walk right out into the brand-new dawn, which was now on the other side of night.

The gate *creak*ed as I pushed it open.

PART ONE: FIRST CONTACT

CHAPTER ONE: FROM THE PERSONAL JOURNAL OF LORENZO ANDRADE.

May, 1519 AD
The Renaissance Period
Southern Italy, Europe

Not sure why I'm going back to when it all started. But it couldn't hurt. Every story has to start somewhere. And this one begins here.

Although, just to let you know, other voices will take over the story at certain points.

But yes, way back in the depths of time, five hundred years ago from the old house, to be exact, was when all this first started.

Who could have known what was set in motion on that idyllic spring evening in the Year of our Lord 1519? Certainly I could not have chosen a more picturesque place to begin my apprenticeship as a blacksmith, in a monastery right on the shore of the Mediterranean Sea, nearby the small village of Terracina. I was, at the time, only a boy of 19.

Oh, my manners. Forgive me.

My name is Lorenzo. I cannot remember the rest of my inherited names, as they, too, are lost to the depths of time. Perhaps someday, once this adventure is over, I might get permission to revisit the time of my life and find out, and put my full name in this journal.

But I remembered that fateful day as if it had happened yesterday.

I was taking my evening stroll along the sandy white sea shore, just as I usually did, taking in a truly glorious sunset, staining the horizon warm red and fading through various colors like a layer cake, until, near the top, the sky was a delicate, nearly transparent shade of purple.

Soon that light show would fade from the sky, leaving only velvety midnight blue behind. Perhaps the stars would be just as glorious, if there were no moon tonight.

But my contemplation of the sunset was disturbed by the sound of rapid footsteps coming up behind me.

"Master Lorenzo." The voice was male, and sounded rather out of breath.

I stopped and turned around. Rapidly approaching was Father Ferrari, the most senior monk at the monastery. He was a man of middle age, as I remembered him, tall and solidly built, with a full head of salt and pepper hair and the usual olive-toned complexion.

"Father Ferrari," I said, bowing in respect.

"My son, I need to speak with you," he said, sounding agreeable and not urgent at all.

"What is it, Father?"

"I know sunset is when you like to take your stroll, and tonight's is an ideal one, if ever there was one. But I have a task I must ask of you."

"Of course, Father. What is it?"

"Well, tonight, in the village, is when they have their bible study class. I'm afraid the monk that usually visits them has come down sick, or so he says."

"Do you think he's faking being sick?"

"Regardless of what I think, we need to bring the Lord's light to those who blindly stumble along in the darkness, and so I must ask you to proceed to the village this evening and give the weekly class. Would you mind terribly, my lad?"

"Not at all, Father," I said agreeably. "Except, are there no other monks to send? After all, I am only a blacksmith, not a monk."

"My son, to hear you speak, you can teach a bible study better than I could. What do you say?"

"I have not been in the village since I first came to the monastery. I would love a chance to see it for the first time."

"There's a good lad," said Father Ferrari, clapping me on the shoulder. "Take one of the horses and proceed to the village right away. I believe you'll just be able to make it."

"At once, Father." I went to the workshop, collected my Bible, and proceeded to the stable to get one of the horses.

In no time at all I was headed to the village.

My poor horse was rather out of breath by the time I arrived at the small school, on the far side of the village from the monastery. I had ridden right past the village, along the beach, and arrived at the school if not on time, then only a minute or two late. By this time night had fully fallen, and, just as I had anticipated, the stars that evening were truly a sight to behold.

But once again, I looked away from my contemplation of the night sky and turned my attention to the tiny schoolhouse instead, as I brought my sturdy beast to a halt and swung down from the saddle.

Like many buildings in the village, it was built quite plainly, of wood and stone. The building was one story, and one room, for that matter, for that was all the village needed. The school bell was oddly silent. Built in an arch overhanging the entrance, it had a long rope hanging down, enabling even a short person to easily ring the bell, calling children to school or parents to church.

Nobody was ringing the bell. *Hmmm.*

Nobody was coming out to meet me, either, as I would have expected, since I was arriving a little bit late. I also would have expected to see people loitering about, that or any people arriving later than I.

But there wasn't a soul around.

Also, the night was entirely too quiet. The evening breezes were the only sound to be heard, besides the Mediterranean. No crickets chirping. No owls hooting, from the trees nearby.

There were, in short, none of the usual night sounds.

And my poor horse was fidgeting. He was shifting on his hooves, making quiet but anxious neighing noises, tossing his head.

"It's all right. There's a good lad," I said quietly, patting its equally sturdy flanks reassuringly. "Do not worry, I shan't be long. Then we can both go home." I tied him to a nearby post. Then I took another good look around. Nothing was obviously amiss. But *something* wasn't right. I could *feel* it.

Thinking that perhaps Father Ferrari had the wrong night, or that maybe the villagers had left before my arrival, I approached the front door of the schoolhouse very carefully, indeed. Loose gravel *crunch*ed under my boots as I crossed the courtyard.

I'm not sure what prompted me to do so, but I reached inside my tunic, feeling for the tiny gold cross my mother had given me, hung on a fine-gauge gold chain, and pulled it out so it hung against the dark brown fabric of my tunic. It was a warm spring evening. I had on no other garment over my tunic, no waistcoat, coat of arms or other such garment.

And then I felt it—quite all at once, and quite strong—a premonition of danger, the urgency of which nearly made me quail. Perhaps, knowing what I know now, I might have chosen a different path that night. I certainly could have turned around, mounted my horse once again, and headed straight back for the workshop. Nobody would have found fault with that, not even my horse.

But I opened that damned door.

Fortunately I didn't just open it. That might have been the end of me. Instead I pulled the door open and stood to one side as if I were holding it for someone. That struck me as odd as well as unnecessary, but did it anyway.

A few moments later, *someone* certainly came out the door.

I can only imagine what she must have looked like while normal—beautiful, or one would have hoped. But the creature that came out of the schoolhouse was anything but beautiful.

It only appeared human, whatever it was. Her skin, pale as parchment paper, had an unnatural glow. The hair, blonde or a similar shade, appeared as if she had been struck by lightning. She was attired in some garment resembling the tattered remains of a white dress.

And that was what she looked like from behind.

All I wanted at that point was to get out of there before she sensed me, but I was at a loss as to how to do that without attracting her attention.

Terrified, I watched her proceed across the courtyard, wiping blood off her face and smearing it along the back of her arm. I was afraid she would be helping herself to my horse next, and that I would be walking home, but in the next moment—she turned around and saw me. The prospect of walking home became the least of my worries.

I froze, my feet seemingly rooted to the ground, as I finally got to see what she looked like from the front. At that moment, I decided ignorance was bliss.

But it was too late now.

The eyes were what was the most frightening to behold. They were red as if with blood, filling the entire eyeball so that it was the only color. And the fangs, unnaturally long, were bright red as well, dripping with what I could only assume was blood. I shuddered.

What abomination was this creature?

I will admit, I was terrified beyond my ability to think. I had never seen such a frightful monster before, and had no name for it.

She gave up a hideous laugh. "Well, what have we here? It seems you were a little late!"

The only thing I could think of was to grip the gold cross I wore.

"I could certainly use an appetizer," she said, her eyes lighting up. "Your friends in there made a lovely dinner. But I'm still a little *hungry*."

And just like *that* — she *charged* — crossing the courtyard in an instant, mouth open as if to bite, the fangs extended, the tips glinting, the eyes frightful to behold. The only thing I could think of was to raise my cross as a shield —

"*Aaaaahhhhh!*"

She just as quickly backed away from me, showing off a faintly smoking burn mark on her left shoulder, in the shape of a cross, as if she'd been branded.

My cross did that?

Shrieking and wailing, she headed off in some random direction, clearly wounded, in pain and in distress. As she staggered off, night sounds began to return, all at once, as if my ears had been plugged but were now unplugged.

Crickets chirped once again. Owls hooted.

I'm sorry to say, that, once she was gone and the danger had passed, I collapsed to my knees, then to the ground, on all fours, and threw up. I was so relieved at not having been the latest meal for that grim creature, whatever she was. After a few moments, I picked myself up off the ground, dusting off my trousers.

That was when I saw him.

He was quite tall, at least six feet if he was an inch, taller than I, dressed in unusual garb, all in black. I couldn't have told you what it was, but I recognized the sturdy boots, as well as a long black coat and a knapsack or pouch of some kind, with the strap slung over his shoulder. He was also broad across the chest and shoulders, and had a bald head.

It was as if he'd appeared out of thin air. I hadn't heard him approach.

"Nice work," he said, in a perfectly calm voice.

I went to the well nearby and rinsed my mouth out with a drink of water. "You mean throwing up, or getting rid of . . .that creature?"

The man cracked a faint smile. "That was a vampire," he said by way of explanation. "That monster you just encountered."

"Ah," I said. "And what, pray tell, is a vampire?"

"I'll spare you the details, but a vampire is a monster that feeds off human blood. They only hunt at night because they cannot handle daylight."

"Ah, I see," I said, unable to think of anything else to say. "Does this . . .vampire . . .even have a name? At all?"

"Yes. Her name is Tasia. I'm very sorry I wasn't here in time to help. I could have stopped her before she crashed the church service."

"What does that mean?" This man spoke the strangest English I'd ever heard. I'd had to learn English because Father and Mother often had to take a ship to England in order to attend to business matters, but this had to be the most unusual English I'd ever heard from anyone's lips, full of words I'd never heard before.

He chuckled. "Getting in when she wasn't invited."

"Tell me," I said urgently, rushing over to him. "Did she bite me? If she bit me, end me now. I don't want to end up like that."

The man lifted my chin to have a good look at my neck. "No. You are fortunate that she did not get you." He let go of my chin. "Your congregation in there, however, was not so lucky."

I turned back towards the schoolhouse, remembering the people inside—

"You don't want to go in there."

"Why not?" I asked.

"Trust me. You don't want to see what's in there. In fact . . .excuse me for a moment." He stepped away from me, pulling something out of his coat pocket and having a short, terse conversation, full of strange words I'd never heard before.

I thought I heard the words *containment* and *cleanup*.

Before I could ask what that was all about, other people began appearing out of thin air, about a dozen of them, all dressed from head to toe in vaguely medical clothes in some baggy, shapeless blue or green material.

Wait! How was this happening?

Next to me, the stranger was chuckling deeply. "Just wait here with me."

As they approached the schoolhouse, I shuddered to imagine what could have been so horrible that I didn't want to see it. Then, remembering my own experience from just moments ago, I stayed out in the courtyard.

"Well now," the strange man said. "We need to decide what to do with you, my friend."

"Sorry," I said. "But I'm not your friend."

"You fought off the vampire," he said. "That makes us friends, in a way."

"All right," I said, conceding the point. "And why do you need to worry about me?"

"Well, because we don't want anyone in the village to find out what's happened. Your village printing press would have a field day with this. More than likely he would run out of paper."

There was a small pause while he gazed at me openly.

He said, "That really was impressive. You fought off the vampire all by yourself, using only your wits."

"Actually, I used this," I said, holding up the gold cross, glancing at it. It was still pure and unblemished, completely unchanged.

"Ah," said the strange man, nodding. "Crosses have an effect on vampires. You see, crosses are made with a purity of heart, by someone who worships a deity. Vampires, however, are evil spirits of darkness, created by Satan. They can't handle even seeing a cross, let alone touching a cross."

"Ah, I see," I said, remembering the burn mark on her body.

"And, as I said, you did it all by yourself, thinking fast on your feet."

"Thank you," I said. "Although that was mostly luck. I froze up before that."

"Understandable," the man said. "Especially when one has never seen a vampire before. They are hideous to behold when they're feeding."

"Indeed," I said. "She truly was—wait, there are *more*?"

"Yes, I'm afraid so," the outsider replied. "You know, we can teach you how to kill them. Vampires, as well as other monsters of the night."

"Oh, *yes*?" I said, derision coloring my tone. "And how, pray tell, would I pay you back for this wonderful training?"

"Only with your service," the strange man said.

I had to admit, being able to defend myself against one of these vile beings was more than enough reason to take him up on his offer.

"All right," I said, admittedly quite curious by then. "Who sent you? You don't look like any monk I've ever seen."

For the first time, the man truly did smile. "I'm not any kind of a monk." He held out his hand as if to clasp mine in greeting. "Take my hand. Come see for yourself."

I stared at his open hand for several moments, noticing a device wrapped around his forearm.

"I'm afraid this is a one-time offer," the stranger said, as if in reply to my indecision. "When I leave here, I won't be coming back."

At that moment, one of the people in medical garb emerged from the schoolhouse, her face looking pale and drawn, yet also set. She approached the strange man and conversed with him for a few moments in low voices, not even looking at me.

Then he turned back to me. "Well, my friend, I'm afraid this is where we take our leave, unless you've decided to come with me. Or, my colleague here can, uh, modify your memory. Trust me, you wouldn't remember a thing. What do you say?"

Once again, he held out his hand.

Knowing what I know, I might have taken a different path that night. I looked at the woman, who was regarding me the same way a doctor might have regarded an interesting patient, although she also had the tiniest degree of sympathy in her cool blue eyes. She held an object in her hand, pointed at me.

Or, perhaps, I might have done the same thing. I might never know.

I took his hand in the clasp of brotherhood.

The world as I knew it disappeared as white light completely filled my sight.

CHAPTER TWO: FROM THE PERSONAL DIARY OF MARIE SCOTT.

Inter-war Period
September, 1925
San Diego, California, USA, North America

It was an ordinary beginning to an ordinary day. My husband, George Scott, was getting ready for his job at the Navy airplane factory. Thanks to that job we had money, for the first time since we got married. Money to pay our mortgage with. Money to go out with. We were even saving, to buy one of the new motor vehicles coming out.

In short, we were able to afford a comfortable, middle-class lifestyle.

It hadn't been difficult for him to find the job. He'd been in the Navy, so all it took was a referral from a friend who had also been in the Navy, and he was at work the next day.

I followed him to the door, wearing my usual attire while at home doing housework—a blue gingham dress with a drop-waist, which means a waist that fell down around the hips, a hemline past the knee, along with dark stockings and clunky black heels, my dark hair all up in curlers at the moment. I would take them out in a little while.

September had been, as I recall, a fairly warm month. George, a tall, strong man, wasn't wearing much under his drab, gray coveralls as he headed to the door carrying his toolbox, a cap perched on his head in an endearingly lopsided manner.

"You have your trolley fare, dear?" I asked him, wiping my wet hands on my apron.

He gave a smile and a nod.

"Try not to work too hard," I said. "Remember, we have that engagement at the club tonight."

"Oh. Yes. That," he said, a frown creasing his face.

"What's wrong?" Normally I was the one casting doubt.

"I don't know," he muttered. "But something about that place just seems . . .shady."

"It's one of the most stylish clubs in the whole city," I said. "Catherine told me she and Jack always have fun there."

George chuckled. "Jack knows how to have fun no matter where he goes."

I patted his strong chest. "Well, the Taylors are sponsoring us. It would be disingenuous to simply not show up."

A smile finally appeared. "Disingenuous? Is that a new word?"

"Stop it," I said playfully, pressing my hand against his chest. I gave him a kiss. "Try to have a good day. I'll meet you there, okay?"

"Okay," he said, giving me a kiss in return. "Don't be late. Jack is even more of a stickler for tardiness than I am. Remember, we're both Navy."

I rolled my eyes. "Right. How could I forget?"

"And please, remember to change clothes," he said, cocking an eyebrow. "You don't want to show up in a day dress."

"I wouldn't *dream* of it," I said, my tone going sultry.

"Goodbye," he said, heading to the door.

"Goodbye, dear," I said, watching from the front door as he headed down the street for the trolley car to the base, the sun peeking above the horizon.

Just as I closed the door, the phone rang. I quickly crossed the room to the kitchen and lifted the receiver, wondering who this could be calling so early. "Hello?"

"Marie," said a female voice. "How are things, love?"

"Sofia?" I asked.

"Why, yes. Who did you think it was?"

"I wasn't sure," I said. "That's why I asked. And things, as you call them, are going fine. George and I are going to the club tonight."

"Ah, excellent," Sofia said, purring. "So were Edward and I, as a matter of fact."

I hesitated to say anything further about myself and George. I wasn't sure why. Only that I felt that to do so would have been a bad idea.

"I thought you said Edward has to work tonight," I asked her instead, to buy time.

"And so I did," Sofia said calmly. "But it turns out he has tonight off. So, we'll see you guys then, love?"

"Yes, I suppose you will," I said, still hesitant for some reason. Something in the back of my mind was screaming.

But Sofia merely made a pleasant sound. "Excellent. Do remember to come dressed for the occasion, will you?"

"George just bought me a party dress," I said.

"Oh, tell me more. Beads?"

"Yes, black and silver," I reported. "With fringe details at the bottom."

"Beautiful," Sofia said.

There was something in her tone that gave me chills. For some reason I opened the drapes to let in daylight—the sun now fully risen and shining strongly.

"Well, I really must be going," Sofia said, all at once. "I just wanted to check in with you."

"Oh, I see," I said. "I'll see you at the club, I expect."

"You certainly will," Sofia said. "Goodbye."

"Goodbye—"

Quite all at once, she hung up. I was left staring at the receiver, the dial tone playing in my ear. After a moment, I hung up as well.

It was almost as if . . .she could sense daylight through the phone.

Then I shook my head at myself. *There you go again with your silly nonsense.*

The sun was about to set as I climbed down from the trolley, joining the throng of people queuing up to cross the street at the crosswalk.

"Hi, Marie," someone said to me.

Recognizing them but not remembering their name, I said, "Hi!"

"Love the dress, dear," they said. "Headed for the club?"

"Yes," I said. "George and I are having a night out. The Taylors are sponsoring us."

"Oh, how lovely."

"Thank you," I said. "Have a good night!"

And they moved off across the street.

I joined the rush of people crossing the street, tucking my little matching beaded purse under my arm as I walked, my Mary Jane heels clicking along, making sure the glittery headdress was in place properly.

Just as he'd promised, my husband George was waiting for me on the opposite side, looking dashing in his topcoat, black hat and tails, his shoes as shiny as only a Navy man could have presented them.

Standing next to him were the Taylors, Jack and Catherine. Jack was George's best friend from his Navy days, who had given him the referral, while Catherine was my friend from our boarding school days. We'd both met our two dashing husbands while at a mixer that had been sponsored by the Navy for the men coming home from the war. Catherine and

I were only 20, you see, while our men were both 25.

While Catherine and I were opposites, her blonde while I was brunette, both of the men were tall, dark, and handsome, although George's face was less symmetrical than Jack's, more rugged.

Catherine said to me, "I really do love this dress!"

"Thank you," I said. "I rather like it. I know George likes it."

The two of us laughed.

Then I said, "You're not looking too bad, yourself."

Catherine winked. "What, this old thing?"

Her dress was much like mine, except it was drenched in glittery golden beads, with a matching hat on over her blonde curls and T-strap heels on her feet.

"Well, the four of us do make a lovely sight," Jack said. "But we won't be doing much of anything standing out here. Let's get inside, shall we?"

"Sounds good to me," George agreed.

I shared a private glance with Catherine as we all headed to the entrance. She rolled her eyes, but I knew she was as proud of her Jack as I was of my George.

The doorman stopped us before we could step inside.

"Do you know who I am?" Jack said, sounding vaguely affronted.

"Of course I know," the doorman said. "I *don't* know who these two are."

"They're with me," Jack said. "I'm sponsoring them. That should be good enough for you."

"Yes, of course. You know I have to ask. Have a nice evening." A muscle in the poor man's face twitched as he stood aside and held the door open for us.

"Thank you," Jack said, sounding only somewhat frosty.

As we stepped inside, George said to him, "What was his problem?"

"More than likely he was just making trouble," Jack said in a dismissive manner. "Although I can't imagine what he means by it."

Then he shook it off.

"Come on, guys. Let's go get a drink."

Laughing, the three of us followed him across the smoky room to the bar.

But our moment of happiness didn't last.

"I see they let all sorts in this place," said a male voice, dripping in sarcasm.

"I served in the Navy," Jack said, letting his voice go frosty again, not becoming intimidated in the least. "So did my friend George. What have you done for the country, if I may ask?"

"Edward, stop being so hard to get along with," a familiar female voice said.

I knew the owner of the voice before she stood next to her husband. As she eased past me, her soft, bare arm sensuously sliding against mine for a brief moment.

The club disappeared—

I was crossing a . . .courtyard?

Then I was inside a schoolhouse. People were screaming as I bit hard into their necks and sucked for all I was worth, feeling their lives ebbing away in between heartbeats, moving as quickly as I could to the next person and the next. Soon there was nothing left but a roomful of dead, dried-up husks that used to be . . .people.

For just a moment, I got the echo of a name—*Tasia*. That was strange. She always said her name was Sofia.

I got a sudden glimpse of a man holding a cross. The glimpse was just that, a glimpse, very momentary. But he was a strong, young man, with dark hair. Then white light filled my sight, followed by unimaginable, lancing pain, followed by a scream.

—and I was back in the club. The transition was very disorienting and disconcerting. I clutched my husband's arm tightly with the abrupt return to the here and now.

"What's wrong?" he whispered.

"Nothing," I whispered in return. "Don't let us get separated."

"I won't," he promised.

Sofia—or was it Tasia—stood next to her husband, looking blonde and beautiful, her hair worn in a short style, wearing a dress all in glittery, sparkly black beads that set off her remarkably pale skin, not to mention her baby-blue eyes.

She looked almost ordinary. Normal, even.

But I couldn't quite relax around her, or her husband. They both creeped me out. Perhaps it was just a trick of the light, but I thought I saw a flash of *red* in Sofia's eyes. For a moment, it crossed my mind that I only saw her at night, either early in the morning or late in the evening, any time before sunrise or after sunset.

Who knew? Maybe she worked third shift at the switchboard.

Then I spied what looked like a burn mark on her shoulder, in the shape of a small *cross*. I almost let out a gasp of recognition, but stopped myself, clapping my hand over my mouth only just in time.

"That must have hurt," I said.

"What must have hurt?" Sofia asked.

"That," I said, gesturing to the scar on her shoulder. "Looks like a burn."

"Oh, that," Sofia said carelessly. "I don't even remember how I got it."

I'm sure you don't, you little tart.

In the meantime, Edward was attempting to smooth things over. "We've all done our part for America during the great war. I thought I heard someone mention drinks? How about if I start things off? The first round's on me."

Well, who could say no to that? Soon the six of us each held a drink in our hands. How this place managed to get away with serving alcohol with Prohibition in effect I did not understand and did not know, and it was probably best not to be too curious.

Then, as we all *clink*ed our glasses together, Sofia said, "You know, we reserved a private room for tonight. How about you all join us? We'd love to have you."

The way she said that sounded . . .wrong.

"That's very kind of you," Jack was saying. "But I don't think the ladies are in the mood for that sort of thing tonight."

"Nonsense," Sofia replied. "I'm sure the ladies would love to get out of all this smoke. Catherine? Marie? Am I the only lady here?"

Cathy and I exchanged uneasy glances. I knew what Cathy was thinking—that none of this felt right in the slightest, that her instincts, like mine, were urgently telling her not to let her get into a room with Sofia, and that I didn't like the glint in Sofia's eyes.

I took that moment to locate the cross I was wearing, a simple cross made of white gold, hung from a matching chain. My grandmother had sworn by that cross. As a little girl I'd heard many stories from her of fighting off vampires with it in her native Romania.

I hadn't believed it for a second—at the time. Now I wasn't so sure.

Quite out of nowhere, Jack said, "Well, I suppose it wouldn't hurt, for just a minute."

Cathy said, "Just for a minute."

So, there we were, in the room Edward and Sofia had reserved.

Right away, as soon as we entered, all my instincts were

shouting at me to get the hell out of there and take my husband and my friends with me. I took my husband's hand like I would never let go and held it firmly, slipping my fingers between his.

He whispered, for the second time, "Marie. *What's wrong?*"

"I don't know," I whispered back. And that was the truth.

There was nothing obviously wrong about that room. There were no mirrors. Everything was in dark, muted colors. There were no torches on the wall or a fireplace, just electric lights, one on each wall and a chandelier hung from the ceiling. And there was padding on all the walls.

There was nothing obviously wrong, as I said. But everything I could see was telling me that I was walking into a trap.

And the worst part? I couldn't tell you how I knew—only that I knew.

We had to get out of there.

Meanwhile, George said, "Yes, well, something is wrong. You're acting like a cat on a hot tin roof. For all the wrong reasons."

I winked at him, mostly to buy time for myself. Then I got an idea.

I made a big show of checking my watch. "George, honey, don't we need to be going? Didn't you say you had a meeting tomorrow at work?"

George met Jack's eye for just a moment, ever so swiftly. "You know what, Jack? Marie is right, you and I do have a meeting in the morning. We all have to go. Sorry, Edward. See you later, Sofia."

"*No. Don't go.*"

I turned—

Sofia looked different. A lot different.

Gone was the glamorous flapper girl. In her place was a hideous creature out of someone's worst nightmares. The lustrous, platinum-blonde locks were replaced by a halo of jagged tufts of hair. Her eyes had turned completely red. And her mouth was full of razor-sharp, wickedly pointed fangs.

Then she rounded on George.

All at once, Sofia took George in an impossibly strong grip, yanked his head back, opened her mouth wide and sank her fangs into his neck. George, my beloved husband, spasmed horribly, then went limp before my eyes.

Cathy screamed.

Sofia turned to me next, mouth open as if to bite. But I raised my cross directly in her path.

"*Aaaahhhh!*" Sofia shrieked, the sound loud in the small room.

Quite all at once, two people materialized in the room out of thin air. "You won't be hurting anyone else, Tasia. Halt."

Laughing and howling in pain all at once, she whirled on the spot and was gone in the blink of an eye, leaving Edward standing there all by himself, looking gob smacked because she had apparently just left him.

Out of nowhere a crossbow *twang*ed, sending an arrow plunging right into Edward's chest. With a scream he instantly flashed into nothing. The arrow thudded into the wall, leaving nothing but dust behind in its wake, which slowly floated to the carpeted floor.

Just like *that*.

One of the two new people went right over to George, then just as quickly stepped away.

"What are you doing?" I said urgently. "You can't just leave him!"

The second person, dressed in rumpled blue garb resembling medical scrubs, shook his head. "I'm sorry. Even if I could do an emergency total blood transfusion on him . . .it wouldn't help. He's gone, Miss. I'm sorry. I'm so sorry."

At that moment, the first person said, "Wait right here." And she went over to where Cathy and Jack stood, at that moment frozen in shock, and pointed some kind of device at them, which beeped and flashed.

Cathy and Jack both blinked several times.

The strange woman said, "You've had a marvelous time in here. George and Marie went off somewhere, but they're all right. Go back downstairs and have a few more drinks. Jack was playing poker and is now a millionaire. Don't forget to take these to the cashier."

And she handed Jack a tall stack of purple and blue poker chips, then held the door open for them. Moving like they weren't quite in control of themselves, Cathy and Jack turned and marched from the room.

What the hell?

Once the door closed, the strange woman rubbed her hands together. "Well, that takes care of that," she said. She turned to her partner. "What about him?"

"His name is George," I said, sounding brittle with tears. My whole world had just gone up in smoke, or so it felt.

"Miss," said the man. "I'm afraid this is no longer your husband. That woman you just encountered sucked all his blood out. Your friends, however, were lucky she went for you next. There could have been four victims in here instead of one."

"Yes," said the woman. "And in return for just one victim she now has a nice matched set of cross marks on her. She won't take that very well at all."

"I feel so much better now," I said. All of the last few minutes was catching up to me.

"So his name is George," the woman said to me. "And what's your name?"

"My name is Marie," I said. The room was starting to spin. Everything was starting to catch up to me. I had to hold on to something, preferably a solid object like a wall.

"Marie," said the woman. "Marie."

I looked at her. She, like me, had lustrous brunette hair,

worn in a bob like so many other countless women, wearing a beaded party dress, a fur wrap coiled around her shoulders.

"What?" I asked petulantly.

"I think you need to come with me. You've not only suffered a traumatic event, but your life in this time is effectively over with."

"Are you trying to help me feel better?" I asked sharply.

"No," she said evenly. "Merely trying to convince you it might be easier to come with me and start a new life with us instead of trying to rebuild your shattered life here. There's been an incident here, in a place where they seem to happen a lot. People will talk. No matter how you try to shake it off, people will always wonder."

Damn. She's right.

I wanted to hunt down Sofia or Tasia or whoever she was to the ends of time, and when I caught up, make her pay. But right now, as this strange woman said, I had nothing but a bunch of problems and no easy solutions, including the mortgage on a house and no husband to bring home a check.

"So, who are you, anyway?" I asked.

The woman held out her hand. "Come with me and find out. I can give you a whole new life. A whole new purpose. A whole new meaning."

"What about my husband?"

The man regarded me sympathetically. "I told you, this isn't your husband anymore. He's beyond that. I'll take care of him, I promise."

"Take my hand," said the woman.

I looked at her, and saw she was holding her hand out. However, I hesitated.

Simply put, I didn't care if I was alone and had to take care of myself. However, I was a woman, living in what was still a man's world, where the man was supposed to take care of everything. I could get a job, but people would still ask me why I wasn't married.

"All right." I put my hand in hers.
She touched a button on a little device.
White light filled my sight.

PART TWO: TRAINING

CHAPTER THREE: FROM THE TRAINING JOURNAL OF CADET LORENZO.

When the white light faded out, I found myself someplace else.

At the time I just assumed I was merely in a different place. The air was cool and moist, although the day was bright and sunny —

Wait. Daytime?

My guide, for that was what he had become, merely smiled at my confusion. "All will be answered in due time," he said. "For now, come with me."

I followed him as he entered into a large, white, rather shabby and non-descript building. Inside, it looked every bit like a monastery in. Bare white walls were everywhere, along with ceilings well above my head. Skylights and floor to ceiling windows seemed to dominate. Plus, every direction I looked, people seemed engaged in what definitely looked like training to me. Training with swords, staffs, various other weapons, and sometimes bare-handed combat was taking place, although it was closely monitored by instructors.

I was more than interested by then. Hell, I wanted to join them.

My guide chuckled, but said nothing. Clearly he could sense my constant glancing around. I was, however, unable to do anything more than just glance around. My guide walked rapidly, forcing me to also walk quite fast in order to keep up.

Finally we reached a broad, shallow flight of stairs, curving away to the right, which we began climbing at once.

A few minutes later, only slightly out of breath for my part, we stepped out into a large, circular chamber, lined with low chairs along the wall.

I realized that people were seated in these chairs. There seemed equal numbers of males and females. They all wore the same unusual clothing of my guide.

One of the people spoke. "Andros," said a deep male voice. "I see you have brought a new recruit."

"Yes," said my guide, Andros. "He was able to fight off the vampire Tasia."

Murmuring swept across the room, which had a tone of surprise.

"Tell us, young one," said the voice, after a moment. "You have a name?"

Andros gave me a single nod.

So I stepped forward. "Well, yes. My name is Lorenzo."

"Very well. And Lorenzo, what time period do you come from?"

Time period? "You mean the year?"

"Yes. What year?"

"Ah . . .the year of our Lord, 1519."

More murmuring swept across the chamber.

"Silence," said the voice. "And tell us, Lorenzo, what happened?"

So I recounted the events that had, after all, just happened.

This time, silence was the only reaction.

"Impressive," said the voice. "Most impressive." There was a moment of silence, after which the voice spoke again. "You are going to receive training, young one. Training that will allow you to vanquish these creatures of the night without fear or hesitation. We ask only that you exercise these skills in our service. Do you agree?"

I suppose I could have said anything at this point. But I said, "Yes. I agree."

"Very good." There was the sound of two crisp hand claps. "Erica."

"Yes, my lord?" From somewhere, a female figure approached, quite slim and toned, not an ounce of fat or flab on her body anywhere, attired in a top and pants of some kind, her hair swept up in a bun.

Once again, I heard Andros chuckling, deeply this time. I could only imagine the look on my face. He apparently thought my reaction amusing.

"Erica, this is Lorenzo. He has agreed to join us."

She gave me a nod by way of greeting. No smile, though.

"Please take him through Orientation and Processing, then show him to his room."

"As you wish, my Lord." She turned to me. "Follow me."

"Follow you? Where, pray tell?"

Finally a smile appeared on her lips, a natural one that reached her eyes. "It's all right. Come with me."

"Uh, all right . . ."

Andros nodded to me. "I will see you later, I expect."

"And what will you be doing?"

"Giving my report to the council," he said.

"Report?"

"Yes," he said. "About you. Among other things."

"Oh."

"Try not to have too much fun."

"Right," I said. Without a further word, I followed Erica, trying not to be distracted by her physique, eye-catching as it was.

After several more hours, I had finally been led to my room, simply furnished with a bed against the wall, a night stand next to the bed with a lamp, and a dresser in the far corner along with a desk and a chair to the left of the door.

Along the way to my room, I had been supplied with clothes. I wasn't surprised to see that all the clothes I held were either black or dark gray, except for strange white shoes.

I wasn't even sure any of it would fit, but my guide, Erica, had simply given me an enigmatic smile and assured me they would indeed fit.

I just said, "Okay . . ."

And then she said, "Don't worry about the clothes you have on. Just leave them here in your room. They'll be taken care of."

"Uhm . . . okay."

"Have a good night," she said with a smile. "I'm sorry there's nothing to eat at the moment, but there will be breakfast in the morning."

"Okay," I said, ignoring my rumbling stomach. Then I said, "What's that in the corner?"

"Oh, that?" she said. "That's a toilet. Don't tell me, they didn't have them in your time?"

"No," I said. "What's a toilet?"

"No worries," she said, demonstrating how to flush the toilet. Then she had left.

I would have thought that, by now, I'd be exhausted beyond imagination, but instead my mind was whirling with everything I had learned.

I was now a Time Cadet.

You might laugh, but at that moment I took it very seriously. Vampires and werewolves were immortal, I had learned. In order to fight them effectively, one had to be able to travel through time, to be able to meet them when and where they might appear. Made sense.

I had, simply put, been plucked from my own time in order to fight creatures of the night, because of one moment's quick thinking with a cross.

Well, I suppose my fate could have been worse. My father's whole family and most of my mother's had been killed by the Great Plague, having died in ghastly pain and suffering. How I had not joined them was, I now understood, nothing more than dumb luck.

These people seemed to know that already. How exactly, I didn't know.

Perhaps the most eye-opening part of the day was the tour I'd been taken on. The facility I was in was both large and extensive. The training rooms I'd seen on my introduction to the place were just part of the facility. Another building housed the student dorms and student dining hall. Yet another building had the huge library.

A student or instructor could go in there and do research on any subject they wished, as long as they got back to their room by a decent hour, preferably before their next training cycle began. That meant that cadets, at least, were limited in how much time they could spend in the library. And being drowsy or sleepy or otherwise inattentive in class the next day was not allowed, as it was explained to me.

In the meantime, the library was easy to get lost in. The building had two stories, divided in half by a long hallway down the middle. From the hallway, it led off into huge rooms full of nothing but books. Each floor contained sections devoted to a time period. Each section contained ten endless shelves stacked one on top of the other all the way to the ceiling, shelf after shelf of priceless books that I had never had access to before, and was now being encouraged to read.

After what was a long day, indeed, I finally stripped off my old clothes for the last time, starting with the boots that felt like they had become stuck to my feet. I'd been wearing clothes like this with little variation for so long that I was glad to be rid of them.

I pulled on black shorts and turned off the light, after

figuring out how the lamp worked, then finally pulled the covers aside and laid down.

The mattress was pliant, yet supportive, and the pillow was the same.

Incredibly enough, I was asleep in minutes.

Chapter Four: From the training Journal of Cadet Marie.

The white light faded out.

I was no longer in the night club. No longer in San Diego.

Where I was . . .I couldn't have said. Somewhere not too far away was the sound of ocean waves and seagulls.

My escort, or whatever she was, said, "Are you all right, my dear?"

"Right now, I don't know what I am, or even where I am," I said sourly.

"Come with me," she said, completely unruffled by my attitude.

Before I could say anything in protest, she started up a short path, which led to a large white building with more glass that I would have thought was possible.

Inside, it was spacious and airy. Ceilings were well over my head. Sunlight beamed down through skylights. Everywhere I looked, people were practicing, with weapons like swords, but also various other weapons, or even hand-to-hand, although an instructor was never far away.

In still other areas, people were practicing flexibility drills with gymnastics or yoga, sometimes both, then finishing off with meditation.

But I also had to keep pace with my guide as she strode across the floor. I barely had a chance to even glance at what was going on if I didn't want to get left behind.

I puffed to keep up. "If you don't mind me asking, where

are we going?"

The woman wasn't even breathing hard. *The tart.* "Not too much farther. I promise."

I continued following her past all the practice areas, and finally we got to a sweeping staircase of broad, shallow steps, curving to the right.

We started climbing. Oh, did I mention I was still in heels?

But I wasn't going to say anything, if for no other reason than I didn't want to show weakness in front of my guide, who was wearing the same style of shoe I was and wasn't saying a thing.

After just a few minutes, we finally emerged into a large, circular room with seats along the rim of the room. All the seats were filled, making me feel as if there was a spotlight on me. My guide and I walked over to a large circle painted on the center of the floor.

The paint of this marking was chipped and worn, indicating many people had stood in this very same spot.

At that moment I realized one chair in the very middle of the row was higher than the others, occupied by a man.

"Lauren," he said, in a calm, deep voice. "Who do we have here?"

"Council members," she said, with a single nod. "This is Marie Scott. She has just had an encounter with the vampire Tasia."

Muttering passed through the room.

"So, Marie, is it?" he asked me.

"Yes," I said.

"Tell us, what time do you come from?"

That question threw me off, but I said, "Nineteen twenty-five."

"And please, tell us, young one, what exactly happened?"

I recounted the events in the private room, as much as I could remember. When I was done, I could hear more muttering.

"Well, that was impressive," said the man. "I agree with Lauren. That situation could have gone worse than what it did. So much worse. But it didn't, thanks to your quick thinking and situational awareness."

I didn't know what that meant, but I nodded. "Thanks. I think."

There was a pause.

"Well, Marie, I also agree with Lauren that it would be a terrible idea to take you back to your time period. So we are going to provide you with training. All we ask in exchange is that you use this training in our service. Do you agree?"

I didn't know what to say. All the activity I saw downstairs made me curious.

I decided it was best for me not to think too much.

So I said, "Yes, I agree."

"Excellent," he said. Then he clapped his hands twice.

From somewhere off to the left, a female figure approached, tall and slender, almost regal, her skin a deep rich chocolate brown, her long, straight black hair slicked back in a ponytail.

"Aisha," said the man. "This is Marie. She has decided to join us."

The woman gave me a single friendly nod, but no smile. "Welcome."

"Thanks," I said.

"Aisha, please take Marie for Processing and Orientation, then take her to her room."

"As you wish," she said, then turned to me. "Please come this way."

I followed her without another word.

A good long while later, I followed Aisha down a long hallway and stopped at a door, which she opened for me, reaching inside to snap on a lamp. "After you, sweetheart."

"Thanks," I muttered, and strode inside, carrying a bundle of clothing, most of which was either black or dark gray, but also appeared soft and comfortable, with a pair of white sneakers resting on top.

I dropped that bundle on the bed and turned around. The room was simply furnished. There was a bed in the far corner from the door. Next to it, a nightstand with a small lamp. To the left of the door was a desk with another lamp and a chair. Way over in the far left corner was a dresser. Next to that was a door which led to a spanking white bathroom, which at the moment looked like a dream come true.

"So, what now?" I asked.

For a moment, she looked surprised. "Now you have a chance to relax and get changed for bed. I know you must be tired."

I yawned. My body had betrayed me again. "A little bit," I replied, blushing.

Aisha beamed kindly at me. "I'm sorry there's no food for you at the moment, but there will be breakfast in the morning. In the meantime, make yourself comfortable."

"Thank you," I said softly.

With a perfect smile, Aisha closed the door.

All alone with nothing for me to do, I went into the bathroom and started to remove my makeup, then I eased off my heels with a sigh, wiggling my feet and calf muscles. Just a few minutes later I was in my birthday suit, searching through my new clothes for something suitable to lounge in.

Just as quickly I was wearing baggy, dark gray sweatpants and a matching sweatshirt, the material pleasantly soft. I put the rest of it in the dresser.

Then I took stock: of my new circumstances, where I was, the whole nine yards.

I had no idea where I was or even when I was. But I did

know I had new purpose, new direction, and a new life, just as Lauren had told me.

I sat on the bed with my back against the wall and tried not to feel too much. But my emotions, mostly grief, caught up to me in my moment of solitude and stillness. I started to cry. I tried to hold the tears at bay, but they stubbornly refused. My emotions washed over me like water slopping over the edge of a sink and splashing on the floor.

I needed my husband to come hold me, but he wouldn't be able to help me now. That only made me feel worse. I cried myself to sleep.

The wakeup call came rather early, the lights coming on all at once, but I got a chance to actually wake up and get moving and get dressed. Breakfast was a quick, orderly affair, served by an efficient kitchen staff.

Once breakfast was done with, our training class, all fifty of us, I discovered, was marched out in single file to a rather cavernous room just like all the others I had seen. Way in the back of the room was what looked like a giant jungle gym, full of obstacles and red beams of light.

Our instructor was a tall brunette beauty whose hair fell to her butt, tumbling down in a cascade of curls. She introduced herself as Special Agent Tera Banks. Then she gestured to the giant jungle gym.

"This is your first test as Time Cadets. Yes, I know, how can we start you out with a test when you haven't had any training yet?"

Now that you mention it, yeah.

"Well, the vampires we would have you hunt will not stop while you get your act together. Sorry, Cadets. They have no sympathy, and neither do we."

The test was deceptively simple—work our way past the obstacles in order to reach a small ball sitting innocently on a pedestal.

My fellow cadets all muttered among themselves, sounding put-upon. But then I noticed the cadet standing next to me. It was *him*!

I tried not to gasp in recognition, clapping my hand over my mouth to stop myself, but it was him—the person from my vision, in the flesh. And what flesh he had.

He stood about five-foot-ten, standing tall and strong, wearing a tank top and sweatpants, both in black, with white sneakers, with close-cropped short black hair on his head. He had a square forehead, thoughtful eyes and olive-toned skin all over his body.

But I didn't have a chance to introduce myself, not at first.

"Now," said the instructor. "I'm going to call you up alphabetically by your first names. You will each draw a number from this basket, from one to one hundred. We will then call you up according to your *number*."

While the instructor started calling people up, I nudged him with my elbow. He turned his head to look my way. "No pressure, right?" I said.

"Right," he said.

"We'll both get the ball," I told him. "Deal?"

"Deal," he said.

"I'm Marie," I whispered.

"Lorenzo," he whispered in return.

"Nice to meet you," I said.

He cracked a grin. God, he looked so handsome. Then the instructor called his name. His face crumpled when he saw his number. But I didn't have a chance to ask him what number he'd drawn, because I took my turn just a few moments later.

My number was seventy-five, I saw. That meant I would be waiting.

Great.

CHAPTER FIVE: FROM THE TRAINING JOURNAL OF CADET LORENZO.

The very next morning, training promptly began—or so I thought.

My day started quite all at once, when the lights came on, followed by a loud, obnoxious alarm hooting up and down the hallway. Before too long I would become used to it. But that first morning, it was shocking to be woken in such a fashion.

Then my stomach rumbled at me. Once I got dressed, in the clothing that had been provided to me, I followed some other people down the hall in search of breakfast.

I found out that I was just one in a class of *fifty* cadets.

And I also found out we had a test on our very first day.

In my mind, I panicked. Hell, we hadn't even studied anything or taken any training, and now we were expected to take a *test*?

The test appeared to be quite simple—make my way through a course filled with beams of red light and assorted physical obstacles, get past those obstacles, retrieve a small ball sitting innocently on a pedestal, and come back with it.

The beams of light were harmless, more for show than anything, but if one was tripped, an alarm would sound, as the instructor demonstrated.

She told us, "This is your first test as Time Cadets. Yes, I know, how can we start you out with a test when you haven't had any training yet?"

Yes, pray tell, how do we do that?

"Well, the vampires we have you hunt will not stop while you get your act together. Sorry, Cadets. They have no sympathy, and neither do we."

Murmuring and muttering passed through the field of cadets.

"Now," said the instructor, a tall, statuesque brunette, "I'm going to call you up alphabetically by your first names. You will each draw a number from this basket, from one to one hundred. We will then call you up according to your *number*."

Great. That meant the whole class would each get their chance, and nobody would be able to say Cadet Whoever got their chance first because the instructor liked them better.

Meantime, the instructor wasted no time calling cadets up.

I felt a soft elbow nudge. I looked over, to see a perfectly ordinary brunette, just like a hundred other girls I'd seen during my time, her hair glossy as mahogany wood, worn in a short, perky style. Her eyes were enchanting. Depending on how they caught the light, they were either blue as the sky or gray as the sea. She wore a dark gray top and black leggings. "No pressure, right?"

"Right," I muttered.

"We'll both get the ball," she whispered. "Deal?"

"Deal," I said, shaking her hand.

"I'm Marie," she said.

"Lorenzo," I said, out the corner of my mouth.

"Nice to meet you," she whispered.

I cracked a grin at her by way of reply. She blushed.

Just a couple of minutes later, I was called up. My number turned out to be eleven. That meant I wouldn't get to sit and watch and get any hints until after my turn. Oh, well. Guess I would just have to figure it out on my own. I liked it better that way. I was always upsetting my teachers at school by doing things my way, because sometimes that wasn't exactly the correct way.

It wasn't too long before Marie was called up. Her number was seventy-five, I saw when she showed me. I cringed. She was going to be sitting for a while.

Too bad we couldn't trade numbers. Oh well.

And, since my number meant I would be going third, my chance came up rather quickly, because the first two cadets flunked out before they even got halfway through. The second cadet got past the first obstacle only to get tripped up by the next. I was surprised. How hard could it be to get a ball?

Both cadets had been led from the room very gently—never to return.

"Cadet eleven," the instructor called out.

I rose, swallowing, headed over to the starting line. "What happens if I fail?"

She looked me in the eye. "Don't fail and you won't have to find out."

"Right," I muttered under my breath. She made it sound so easy.

"Ready?" she asked.

"Ready," I said, taking a deep breath and letting it out. I'd survived going up against a vampire. How hard could *this* be?

"Three . . . two . . . one . . . go."

To this day I still don't understand how I made it, but I literally took it one obstacle at a time. Here I had somewhat of an advantage. As a child, I'd played in obstacle courses both official and unofficial, both natural and man-made, ever since I could walk or talk.

No, you don't want to know.

Before I knew it, I had that little ball in my hand. Now I just had to make it out. Again, before I knew it, I had eased past that first light beam and rose to a standing position, the ball held proudly in my hand.

The class clapped for me, those who were left.

"Very good," the instructor said, taking the ball from me.

"Please have a seat, Lorenzo."

And I did, very quickly, thankful that was over with.

"See?" Marie whispered. "Piece of cake, right?"

"Right," I whispered back. *Whatever that means.*

Once the pressure was off, it was actually fun to watch the others. I winced with sympathy every time one of them tripped a light beam and had to be escorted from the room while the maze was reset.

By the time Marie's turn came, less than half the class remained. For such a simple test, this was turning out to be brutal.

"Cadet seventy-five," the instructor called out.

"Piece of cake," I reminded her in a low voice.

"Right," she murmured.

I watched her negotiate the maze with cat-like, deadpan aplomb, like it was all no big deal, although she took her time and didn't rush it. Smart girl.

Ten minutes later she also emerged from the maze, tossing the ball in the air and catching it in her hand to applause, before handing it to the instructor, who turned to face us. "Well, cadets, you'll be happy to know that Marie was the last number on the list. Look around. These are the remaining members of your training class. Hopefully we won't lose any more.

"Let's take a break for lunch, shall we? I think you deserve it."

As we all left the room for the mess hall, the instructor came up next to me. "See, that wasn't so bad, was it?"

"Nope," I agreed. "But what would have happened if I had failed?"

"If you had failed, you would have been sent back to your own time that we had recruited you from, as if you never left."

She stated it simply, without fanfare. For a second I wondered how that was possible, until I remembered Andros mentioning having my memory modified if I hadn't chosen to come with him. I was glad I decided to come with him.

"Oh," was all I said. After a moment, I realized what a punishment that would have been. "Well," I said. "Good thing I made it through."

"Yes." She smiled. "Good thing. Now come on, I'm sure you must be hungry."

And the very next day, the actual training started. For real.

Chapter Six: From the training journal of Cadet Marie.

I was happy to see our training class was making progress. Every few months we revisited the laser-beam obstacle course, and each time someone failed. It's always a little shocking, to put it mildly, when a cadet that was blowing everyone away with their technique in this or that, couldn't negotiate a simple obstacle course.

We were now down to fifteen cadets—out of a class of fifty.

However, there was hope. The same dozen or so cadets seem to get through the maze with no problems at all. Including yours truly.

I'm not going to lie. Becoming a Time Cadet has probably been the best thing that could have happened to me, once I got past that first night. I don't mind eating humble pie, although it doesn't taste good.

Every once in a while, I still thought I could have managed on my own. And then I just as quickly came to my senses. More than likely I would have ended up on hard times, bitter and lonely, wondering what could have been. This way I have a potential path to revenge. You could even say it's just a matter of time.

And now love has entered the picture, although it's not that strong, not yet. I don't know how I feel about it.

You can probably guess who it is. Yes, it's Lorenzo.

God, you should see this guy! Compared to how he looked when training started, he looked like even more of a stud now. He's really filled out. Not an ounce of fat on him.

I remember one day last week, when we had a meditation session after a workout. We were all laying on the floor, on mats. There was still an empty mat next to mine. The room was very quiet.

Some cadets didn't like the twenty-to-thirty-minute-long meditation period, feeling like their time was best spent learning the tricks of their trade. However, I loved them.

This particular day we had been concentrating on working out, and this meditation period was the last activity for the day, after which I had every intention of heading to the cadets' lounge for relaxation. I had chosen to do a gymnastics workout. Now I was laid out across a yoga mat, dressed only in a sports bra and tiny shorts, my hair slicked back in a tiny ballerina bun.

I was hot and sweaty and having the time of my life.

As I lay there, my eyes closed, I felt movement next to me. I opened my eyes to discover it was none other than my Lorenzo. I felt my heart swell. Certainly I smiled really wide.

That day Lorenzo had on a black muscle shirt, black shorts, and scrunchy white socks. Once he'd lain down on the mat next to mine, I reached over and lightly scratched his arm to get his attention.

Right away, he turned and looked at me, cracking a grin.

I beamed at him in return. I loved his grins.

Then I stared up at the ceiling, hoping he couldn't see my sudden tears.

God, please, don't let me fall in love. I can't be falling in love again, I just can't, not after what happened with my husband . . .

I felt a tear rolling down the side of my face as I made myself pay attention to my breath. Then I felt a hand on my arm.

I looked and saw Lorenzo gazing at me with warm, concerned eyes. So I patted his arm and nodded, as if to say, *I'm okay.*

He nodded in return, then closed his eyes.

More tears ran down my face, in counterpoint to the warmth that seemed to fill my very being, as I kept staring at the ceiling.

I closed my eyes and surrendered to the warm emotions that filled my heart. If I was going to fall in love, so be it.

Chapter Seven: From the training journal of Cadet Lorenzo.

The last three years have flown by in the blink of an eye. The training I've received has been world-class, and not just in fighting with swords, weapons, and martial arts, but education in world history, astronomy, and most importantly, how to kill a vampire.

That was a pretty interesting class.

As I found out, there were several ways to hurt a vampire. The trick was to use something that was made with purity of heart or purpose. Holy water, used during sacrament services, was one method. Splash it on the vampire and it was smoke city. Another method was to employ a cross. This was more difficult. You had to get close enough to the vampire in question for them to come into contact with the cross. Vampires were best viewed from a distance—a *safe* distance.

There were other methods, including these two, that could hurt a vampire, but wouldn't kill it.

There was only four fool-proof ways to kill a vampire—with a wooden stake to the heart, a beheading, or being exposed to broad daylight, especially brand-new morning sunlight—were all easier said than done. The last method, to light them on fire, wasn't exactly feasible.

A vampire wasn't exactly going to walk out into broad daylight just because I asked it to—to which the instructor had responded, *in class*, quite matter-of-factly, that they would if you asked *nicely*, or if they were so disillusioned or unhappy with the whole vampire lifestyle, that they just wanted to end it all. The trick was to get them to feel guilt or remorse.

That was the vampire's Achilles Heel.

We also learned something new about vampires. There were what were called Primary and Secondary Vampires. Primary Vampires were those that had been personally created by Satan himself, just as God created angels. Primary vampires were often quite powerful, with unexpected powers that made it difficult to kill them. Secondary vampires, however, were created when a Primary vampire claimed a human victim. They were easier to kill. Secondary vampires more often than not simply wanted one thing—blood.

Killing either type of vampire came with its share of risks as well as benefits. At the death of a vampire, any of the human victims it had taken as new vampires would resume their mortal form at the time they were turned. Unfortunately, vampires are also immortal. That meant that potentially decades or even hundreds of years could have passed in between being turned and having the vampire responsible meet their maker.

They could have been anywhere in the world when that happened. Beloved relatives could have been long gone, dead and buried. They might have to get used to a whole new time period.

It goes without saying it had not been the victim's choice to be turned.

Talk about no pressure.

I shuddered, hoping I didn't have that delicate task anytime soon. It was listed as one of the many specialties an agent could train for once they had passed primary training.

Especially with secondary vampires, it was difficult to get them to feel remorse, or much of anything, especially when all they wanted was blood.

Sure. Convince the vampire to walk out into daylight. Piece of cake.

Which reminds me — the one thing I never expected to find during the training was my other half. Yeah, remember that girl I met during that first test? Her first name is Marie. Her last name I never found out. Either she, like me, had forgotten she ever had a last name, or she'd never known it in the first place.

But every time we were paired to study together or train or do some activity that required us to work together, such as practice with weapons, we worked together so well it was as if we were two sides of the same coin.

At this moment, I wasn't sure if my affection was professional in nature or if it was more, shall we say, *personal.*

Especially after the day when we learned how to shapeshift for the first time.

The instructor had been remarkably coy with us that day, calling our class into a rather dark room with hardly any light, just enough to see by, a cavernous room like all the others, with high ceilings.

I wondered, not for the last time, if there were any other kinds of rooms in the building.

But the instructor, once everyone was in the room, said, "Well, cadets, I know this is rather sudden, after you've had a long day of training, but this afternoon you will get your first chance to shapeshift."

Murmuring passed between us.

"Now," the instructor, a solidly built male with a bald head, continued after a moment. "Shapeshifting, or being able to shapeshift, is not an accident. It is a talent you can develop, just like being able to shoot a vampire in the heart with the first shot, for example. It is a weapon in your arsenal, something you can do at the right moment. Like so."

Right before our very eyes, he shifted into a large black panther, paced before us a few times, and just like that, changed back into his human form.

Impressed murmuring passed between us.

Our instructor let the murmuring keep going for a moment. Then he continued, "All right, cadets, let's try and focus, now." He spoke quietly, but with an odd sort of tension in his voice. "Shapeshifting is something that, you're going to discover, is probably one of the most difficult skills you're going to master. But you'll also find, that, once you do master it, it will be effortless. The trick is to get into the right state of mind."

Privately, I wondered what that was. Next to me, Marie was wondering the same thing, judging by the rapt expression on her face.

"We all know why it's important to be able to shapeshift," the instructor continued. "Can anyone tell me why?"

Next to me, Marie raised her hand.

"Yes, Cadet Marie?"

"Because a werewolf can't infect you with its bite."

"Very good," he said. "But that's not the only reason. Can anyone tell me another reason?"

I raised my hand.

"Yes, Cadet Lorenzo?"

"Because only animals have reflexes fast enough to counter a vampire."

"Yes, very good, cadet." In the next moment, the instructor said, "Cadet Lorenzo. Cadet Marie. Would you please step over here and join me?"

Marie and I both went over to stand next to the instructor. I tried not to notice the light sheen of sweat on Marie's body, and what a body she had. She, like me, had been through a hard day of training. Over the last three years, I'd watched her body become much like Erica's — slim and toned, without any fat or flab anywhere on her body.

And I mean *anywhere*.

At the moment, Marie was wearing the standard workout attire, of a dark gray bra top and matching sweatpants, white sneakers on her feet, with her hair up in a tiny bun.

I'd never seen her looking hotter—physically, sexually, and in every other way.

Unfortunately, my dick agreed with me. It was straining against my boxers. The funny thing was, most of the time I was in training, I mostly forgot about relationships. I mean, I became *friends* with my fellow cadets, but as far as having sex was concerned, it didn't cross my mind.

Until now.

It didn't help that Marie was looking incredibly sexy, even though all we'd been doing for the last hour and some was work out and practice with weapons.

"Cadet Marie," the instructor said. "Please step behind these curtains over here."

"Yes, sir," she said agreeably, stepping behind a privacy partition nearby.

For some reason, things got very quiet behind that curtain.

"Cadet Lorenzo," the instructor said. "How would you describe Cadet Marie at the moment?"

"Uhm . . .can I speak candidly, sir?"

The man cracked the tiniest of grins. "Permission granted, cadet."

"Uhm, well, she looks hot and sweaty, sir. Mostly, uhm, hot."

Chuckles issued from the remaining male cadets. All the female cadets giggled.

The instructor merely widened his grin. "Cadet Marie? Could you step out, please?"

Click. Click. Click.

I was temporarily confused. *Wait, she wasn't wearing heels.*

Or hadn't been.

Marie took three steps out from behind the screen. And then she simply stood there, resting her hands on her waist.

I was rendered speechless. Gone were the sweats. And the sneakers. In their place was a pair of white leather thigh-high boots, making Marie look ten feet tall, with miles of legs. And nothing else.

I mean nothing else.

Her body was, simply put, toned in all the right places. And in all the other places, well, I was intent on not looking. Over the course of our training, Marie's appearance had changed in many ways, her body not least of which. Her hair had grown out, so it was now about halfway down her back.

Ladies, you make a big deal about being able to express yourselves. But if you can reduce a man to single words like *damn*, you've done your job as far as looking good is concerned.

That's what I was reduced to. *Damn*. That was the only word that would register.

Marie threw me a knowing smile. She could probably tell for herself exactly what was going through my mind—mostly that I wasn't thinking with my mind.

Marie didn't wait to be told what to do next.

She slowly walked over to me, her eyes half-closed, her mouth half-open. She rested her hands on my chest, leaned in—and kissed me.

Her kiss was full of heat, wanton desire, and *I want you — now*.

She matched action to desire, her action leaving no doubt what she wanted. She eased down, rested her hands on my hips, and eased her fingertips under the elastic waistband of my sweatpants, and eased them down until my cock popped out, fully erect.

A look of pure lust in her eye, she took my cock in her

mouth and went to town on it, sliding her lips and tongue down my shaft and back up again until it was coated in saliva.

I'm not gonna lie. If *primal, animal fucking* was on the menu, I was down with that.

She didn't keep up the action on my dick for long. She released my dick, turned around, bent over, reached back and guided it to her waiting pussy entrance.

All I had to do was push forward. I growled as I entered her, a sandpapery sound full of lust.

Every moment I'd watched her in training, wanting her, came down to this. Her pussy fit like a glove made of molten lava as I claimed her, pushing forward all at once until the front of my hips were touching her ass. I glanced up at the ceiling, closing my eyes.

She made sexy passion noises of her own as I eased inside her, holding that pose for a moment. Then I held her waist and started moving.

"That's *it*," she said, sounding carnal and lustful. "Mmmm. Hmmm."

There we were—fucking. There was no other word for it. And I wasn't being gentle. In fact I was pounding the shit out of her pussy.

Quite suddenly, it happened. My arms and legs both shortened, became stout and muscular, with fur — white fur, to be exact, with black stripes.

I was growling. Literally. Because I was a cat. A big fucking tiger.

Underneath me, Marie had changed into a snow leopard.

I couldn't believe it. We had both shapeshifted into animals. It had just required us to be whipped up into a frenzy of sexual desire to make it happen, all the way up to orgasm.

The moment eventually came, so to speak, then passed. I pulled out of Marie. Then both of us strolled around the room in our feline forms, and finally changed back to human shape.

The rest of our class applauded.

Marie and I were absolutely spent. She gave me a tender, sweaty smile. I cracked a grin at her, even as I tried to get my breath back.

The instructor, meanwhile, said to us, "I think you guys are done for today. I suggest a good, long, cold shower, by yourselves. Get out of here."

"Thank you, sir," we both said, got our clothes back on and headed for our rooms.

The shapeshifting class was several days ago. In that time we both had managed to shift again into our animal forms, although by ourselves was, as I suspected, more difficult.

I found it was easier when I took my mind back to that day and remembered all the sensations, trying not to think too much. Only to feel.

Maybe that was the lesson.

I have to admit, it was much easier for us to actually have sex, and from that place be able to shift, than to take myself mentally to that place.

That was something I was going to have to work on.

Chapter Eight: From the Training Journal of Cadet Marie.

It took a few days before I had the courage to see Lorenzo privately. But I did, eventually.

One evening, after dinner and hanging out in the cadets' lounge for a while, I ventured over to the male cadets' quarters, found Lorenzo's room and knocked on his door.

"Come in," he said.

So I pushed the door open and entered his room. It was, like everyone else's, simply furnished. Bed, nightstand, chest of drawers, desk and chair.

Lorenzo was seated at his desk. At my entrance, he put down the book he was reading and gave me his full attention. He turned away from his desk and faced me.

"Hey," he said.

"Hi," I said softly.

"There's this look on your face that says you're not here for a social visit," he said. "So, what's up, I guess is the question?"

"I haven't been able to stop thinking about you. Not since last week . . ." My voice trembled slightly with that simple admission.

I saw his throat move. "Neither have I," he said quietly.

"I didn't think I would like fucking with you as much as I did."

"Thanks," he cracked. "I think . . ."

I swallowed, too. "No, silly, that was meant to be a compliment."

"Actually, that was pretty awesome."

I giggled. "Listen to you. Back when training first started, you spoke all strange. Now you sound like a surfer."

He chuckled. "Yeah, I have noticed my language has changed. I'm not sure what that means, but it's nice to not get any weird looks anymore."

I winked. "Anyway . . .I have to agree, having sex with you was, like, pretty awesome. I just hope it doesn't have to be that way every time we have to shift."

Lorenzo laughed heartily. "Yeah. That would be awkward in social situations."

I laughed, too. "Yeah. Just a little."

There was a tiny pause while I regarded him silently.

Then I said, "I like you, Lorenzo."

"I like you, too. You're pretty cool."

"Thank you," I said simply. "Hey. Uhm. Do you mind if I give you a hug?"

"Of course not," he said, his tone as if to say, *like, duh, no.*

The only bad thing was, at the moment I was wearing flat sneakers again instead of those sexy white boots I'd had on. All I could do was slip my arms around his waist and rest my hands on his back.

But that was enough.

I rested my chin on his shoulder, closing my eyes, inhaling his scent. I clenched my hands, grabbing his muscle shirt in my hands, pulling it up, until I could touch his back—

It happened in a heartbeat. The room disappeared and—

—it was a dark, misty night. Behind me, the sun was just setting, about to dip beneath the horizon. And dead ahead of me, the moon was just beginning to rise. Both things were happening at the same time.

That scene dissolved.

Just as quickly, several new scenes flashed before my eyes. A gate *creak*ed as I pushed it open. Then I was entering a creepy, old, abandoned house, the kind I wouldn't go into even in broad daylight.

I didn't even have to pick the lock. The door just opened inward, seemingly all by itself.

And then, red eyes were staring at me in the gloom—

—suddenly the room was back.

"Marie!" Lorenzo was shaking me. "Marie, what's wrong? You were screaming."

Just as suddenly I broke down crying, sobbing and gulping air, Lorenzo holding me tightly.

"You had a vision," the instructor on dorm monitor duty was saying a little while later. "Fascinating."

"Yes, I'm sure it was," I said, my voice trembling. "But what do you think it means?"

"Tell me about this vision," he said.

So I did. I told him all I could remember.

"Well, it was obviously a vision of the future," he said, thoughtfully and carefully. "I think we can rule out anything like that happening here. We don't have any vampires hanging around in our training halls."

"Are you sure?" I asked, not so certain.

"Yes," he said, perfectly seriously. Then he gave me a searching look. "Is this a new thing? Or have you had these visions before?"

I gulped. "Well . . .usually when I touch someone for the first time, I have a vision. I never know if it's of their past or their present. This is the first time I've had a future vision. If that's what it was."

"Fascinating," he repeated, looking away, holding his chin. "Never had a cadet with psychic powers before. Most interesting."

"I'm sure it is," I said, rolling my eyes. Nearby, Lorenzo cracked a grin.

Despite myself, I winked at him.

"Well," he said all at once, looking at me. "I can certainly understand how you can be a little shaken. If you like, I can have one of the medics give you a sleeping aid. Very mild, I assure you. What do you say, Cadet?"

I told him I would take the sedative.

Just a few minutes later, I could feel the beginnings of drowsiness. Lorenzo quickly volunteered to take me back to my room. I was ready for that. I wasn't ready for him to scoop me up in his strong arms and carry me back.

I didn't have the vision again that night, or ever again. In fact, I was afraid to even touch Lorenzo after that. But it stayed with me, along with the certain knowledge that the vision could mean the difference between life or death.

The question was—whose life hung in the balance?

Chapter Nine: From the training journal of Cadet Lorenzo.

Final exam time. The last test. I knew it had to be coming soon.

As it had been explained to me and the remaining members of my training class, we had each gotten to a place in our skills that we were able to take down the craftiest, most wily master instructors in each of the areas in which a cadet had to display mastery — physical fitness and dexterity, knowledge and use of weapons, with emphasis allowed on one weapon, and what they called other skills, which could have meant anything else, such as shapeshifting. In Marie's case, her psychic powers would certainly count. I'd been pondering that vision of hers.

I had no idea what it could have meant. Apparently it was a vision of the future, but beyond that, I could not imagine what bearing it might have or even how I would eventually get in that kind of a situation.

There was no sense in getting worked up about it. But I would definitely keep it in mind.

I made it sound like no big deal, but out of my training class of fifty, only eleven cadets were left, including myself and Marie—five male and six female. I had been told by one of the instructors that was actually a high number, after expressing my concern one day that there were so few of us remaining.

That didn't exactly calm my fears.

The night before the big final exam, I was tossing and

turning in my bed, unable to get to sleep. I had been thinking all day about what it would be like to be an agent. Then that started me thinking about the test. And what would happen if I failed.

I tried not to think about that. Instead I recalled the words of advice that female instructor had given me on that first day—"Don't fail and you won't have to find out."

Yeah. Great.

Then I got started thinking about Marie. If I failed the final test tomorrow, not only would I never see her again, but I wouldn't even remember her. All that would be erased.

I had to pass tomorrow. I had to.

Incredibly enough, I finally fell asleep.

The next day after breakfast, the eleven of us were led to a room we realized we had never been to, where another instructor greeted us. "Good morning, cadets.

"You, out of all your fellow cadets, have consistently scored the highest, and generally done the best.

"But now it all comes down to this. Your final exam."

And in the back of the room, an enormous black canvas was removed.

"I'm sure you all recognize this," the instructor said with a smile. "Yes, this was the test we had you take the very first day of your training. What better way to end your training than the way you started? However, there's a catch. This time, we expect you to employ any of the skills you have learned during your training.

"It can be anything—a greater store of patience, or an even greater degree of flexibility or dexterity. The point is to pass this test all over again, using any of the skills you have learned since training started.

"Don't get too confident. Just like with the first test, if you trip one of these laser beams, well, you know what will happen."

Yeah. Instead of graduating, you get shown to the door, have your memory zapped, and you will be dropped off in your original time and place like you never left, with a neat, tidy and sensible explanation why you weren't where everyone thought you were.

"And now, cadets, just as before, I'm going to call each of you up by your first name. You will draw a number, from one to fifty. Once you each have a number, you will be called by your number."

And he called the first cadet.

The first time I took the test, it wasn't too difficult at all. Not easy, but not difficult, either. This time around, it was ridiculously easy.

Once it was my turn and I had to concentrate, all my fears fell away and I was soon slipping in between those laser beams like a shadow. Those three years of physical training, gymnastics, martial arts and weapons training had been good for me.

Seven and a half easy minutes later, I stepped through the last laser beam, straightened up and simply handed the ball to the instructor.

"Congratulations, Agent Lorenzo."

"Thank you, sir." I couldn't help it. I cracked a goofy grin.

"If you wish, you may stay to watch your fellow cadets. Otherwise you may conduct yourself as you wish. We will come find you when the last cadet has taken their turn."

"There's not that many left," I said easily. "I'll stay and watch."

"Very well," he said. "Please take your seat."

Right after my turn, Marie was next.

CHAPTER TEN: FROM THE TRAINING JOURNAL OF CADET MARIE.

I can hardly believe it. Three years have just flown by. It hardly seems like three years. But here I am. In the morning I'm going to take the final exam, whatever that is.

I'm not even going to speculate on what form that test might take. Who knows, it could just as easily be a multiple-choice quiz as anything, but I doubt it.

It's a pity that my husband is no longer alive to see me as I am today, although he might not have recognized me. Sometimes I don't recognize myself. Physically, my hair is longer, and my body is more supple and toned than I could have dreamed of. I could go back to the Roaring Twenties and try on any dress I wanted.

I've taken yoga, tai-chi, meditation, gymnastics, and at least two martial arts, plus I've taken classes, about world history, the linear nature of time, and philosophy. My mind has been opened up, as well as my body.

Possibly the most interesting class was on how to kill a werewolf, which was even more interesting than how to kill a vampire. With a werewolf, there was only one thing to be done, and that was to kill it, usually with a silver-tipped arrow from a crossbow, or a silver-tipped ballistic projectile from a pistol or other type of weapon.

I've become quite good at shooting with such weapons.

Tomorrow, I plan on graduating. And when I do, I'm going after the hussy who took my husband's life. I'll readily admit,

I've found it hard to move past my husband's death. Although it hasn't been so much his death, but also the death of my perfectly fine life — the kind of life some might reject out of hand as being too normal, but I had been perfectly happy with, thank you very much.

I remember it was a shock when I went to the library one evening after dinner and read about the time I had been rescued from. It was referred to as the Roaring Twenties, the decade after the First World War, known as much for living excessively large as anything else—until it all came crashing down in 1929 with Black Tuesday, the stock market crash in October of 1929, to be specific, leading to the Great Depression.

I might not have had my perfect little life for much longer, but if it hadn't been for that vampire, I would have still had it. In a way, I feel responsible. After all, I had been the one to insist on going to that stupid night club.

Then there's Lorenzo. Dear, sweet Lorenzo.

I'm not going to lie — I haven't forgotten the day we both learned how to shapeshift. Apparently one has to be whipped up into a state of sexual arousal in order to shapeshift the first time, so that one can recall that memory later and use it to shapeshift on command if it became necessary.

Lorenzo was the first man to take me since my marriage.

And *oh*—how he took me. I've never been so thoroughly fucked as when Lorenzo put his cock in my pussy.

That was the first time that I'd experienced sex on that level — it wasn't lovemaking or even just fucking, it was animal copulation. The only difference between us and two animals mating was the species.

I got an electric thrill every time I thought about it. I shuddered and got wet all over again. I could feel my inner animal under the surface, just itching to come out.

Of course, that was nothing compared to having that

vision. Even though I haven't had anything close to it since then, I've thought about that vision every day since then.

I'm still not sure what I'm going to do, with or about Lorenzo. What I do know for sure is that I'm ready to graduate. I'm ready to be an agent.

I'm ready for revenge.

The very next morning, after breakfast, the eleven of us were taken without explanation to a room that, I realized, we had never been to. It was a room that, like all the others, featured high ceilings, but the corners were lost to darkness, and way back in the back was something covered with an enormous black canvas.

I thought I knew where this was heading. I swallowed with anxiety.

Then the instructor addressed us. "Good morning, cadets.

"You, out of all your fellow cadets, have consistently scored the highest, and generally done the best.

"But now it all comes down to this. Your final exam."

And with that, he pulled a rope, causing the canvas to come down.

"I'm sure you all recognize this," the instructor said with a smile. "Yes, this was the test we had you take the very first day of your training. What better way to end your training than the way you started? However, there's a catch."

Of course there is.

"This time, we expect you to employ any of the skills you have learned during your training.

"It can be anything—a greater store of patience, or an even greater degree of flexibility or dexterity. The point is to pass this test all over again, using any of the skills you have learned.

"Don't get too confident. Just like with the first test, if you trip one of these laser beams, well, you know what will happen."

I gulped again. I knew. I had already seen it happen with other cadets the previous times we had taken this test. I knew I didn't want it to happen to me.

"And now, cadets, just as before, I'm going to call each of you up by your first name. You will draw a number, from one to fifty. Once you each have a number, you will be called by your number."

Being that there were only eleven of us, it didn't take long for us to draw numbers. In fact, I was very nearly in the middle of the field, right behind Lorenzo.

Lorenzo . . .

As I drew my number, I was hoping for something random like 13 or 27, just to shuffle the order around, but my number was 35, only a few numbers behind Lorenzo's. At least I wouldn't be going last this time, although I was pretty far back.

As everyone else before me went, I deliberately didn't watch. I didn't want to see anyone fail, right before graduation. So I spent the time in deep meditation. Incredibly, everyone had made it through safely, so far. I looked up just in time to see Lorenzo hand the ball to the instructor, grinning his ass off.

The obstacle course was reset, the ball returned to its place.

Then it was my turn.

"Cadet thirty-five."

I approached the starting line, gathering my hair up into a bun as I did so. Doing that was also my way of gathering up my mind.

As he did before with all the others, he said to me, "Remember, cadet, you have to employ any of the skills you have learned in order to reach the ball and return it to me. You have no time limit. Ready?"

I gave a single nod. "Ready, sir."

"Okay. Three. Two. One. Go."

And I started wending my way through the course. I took a more conservative method than my fellow cadets. While others took the direct route to the ball, I passed up obvious openings and took a more careful path to the ball.

Even so, it wasn't as bad as I feared. I found the gymnastics and yoga training most helpful here, allowing me to pass by, around, or through obstacles like a whisper.

Twenty minutes later, quietly triumphant, I handed the ball to the instructor. "Very good, *Agent* Marie. Congratulations."

"Thank you, sir."

"Go have a seat with the others."

"Yes, sir." I could feel myself glowing from the inside out as I resumed my seat with the others who had also passed. Lorenzo and I exchanged a high-five.

"Good job," he whispered.

"Piece of cake," I said confidently.

The line-up had been shuffled to some degree, so that Lorenzo and I were towards the end, although we had both been in the middle, alphabetically. So once I had completed the obstacle course, there were only two more cadets, who both passed.

The rest of us greeted the last cadet, who was now a new agent, with cheers and hugs.

Then the instructor addressed us again. "Well, congratulations, agents. I'm happy to see you have all passed. Tomorrow you will get your first assignments, but today you get to celebrate. Feel free to pass the rest of the day as you like, but this evening there will be a mixer to attend. You will be expected to dress appropriately. Just try your best not to let it get out of hand."

We all laughed.

"You are all dismissed from training. Once again, congratulations."

As soon as he said that, we all jumped up, laughing and cheering, hugging and kissing everyone in sight.

But this wasn't the end. It was the beginning.

You're mine, Tasia. I'm coming for you.

PART THREE: TARGET ACQUIRED

Chapter Eleven: From the personal diary of the Vampire Tasia.

The Second World War
Somewhere in Nazi-Occupied France
June 1, 1940

The doctor gave me a piercing stare over the top of his wire-rimmed glasses. "These burn marks must have hurt," he said in a cultured German accent.

I batted my baby blue eyes at him. "I'm afraid I'm ever so clumsy," I said, in a fake but otherwise plausible French accent. "Isn't there anything you can do about them?"

"There might be," he said, peering closely at them. "One of them looks quite old. However the other one looks more recent. That one I should be able to remove completely."

"Of course," I said, sighing theatrically. "Do what you can with them. I'm sure you'll agree they are quite unsightly."

"Indeed," he said. "They look like you were branded with something."

I winced with the memory. Vampires have long memories, and I wouldn't soon forget the two instances where a human prey in my sights has been able to fight back against me.

That has happened only twice, I assure you.

The others have not been so fortunate. Like that church service I happened upon in southern Italy, so long ago, not too long after I was bitten. Before I got the first cross burn, I was able to suck them all dry. Sometimes, just when I think I might make a new vampire, the taste of blood gets the better of me and I just keep sucking until there's nothing left but a dead, dry husk.

That's what happened at that night club in San Diego, too. I got so impatient with trying to get those four people to relax and not be so suspicious, that I just bit into that man's neck and went to town. I couldn't help myself. There wasn't much left of him when I was done.

But I paid for that moment of ecstasy. The woman with him had that damned cross with her, and she knew how to use it.

The doctor's next words brought me back to the here and now. "I won't be able to remove them entirely, but I'll do my best. We need to have you be able to blend in."

"As I said, do what you can. I'll be very happy either way."

A faint pink tinge appeared in his cheeks. "Lie back for me, dear. If you feel any discomfort, do not hesitate to tell me."

The very next day I met with an older officer, a seasoned, experienced man who seemed to know what he was talking about.

"All right, listen. We're going to have you going into London. A pretty young thing like yourself shouldn't have much trouble catching the eye of a Royal Air Force officer."

I smiled. I was hardly young. But I still looked it.

"Your mission is clear. Find out how many squadrons they have. We have an incomplete picture, and we need to know more. Any questions?"

"No," I assured him.

"Good. Do try to work as quickly as possible, but not so quickly that you arouse suspicion. The Fuhrer wants to be in London by the end of summer. Once England is neutralized, we can take our time with Russia."

"Leave it to me," I said.

"Get ready," he said. "You leave for your mission tomorrow. I suggest you get your affairs in order. Just in case."

"It won't be a problem," I said.

British blood tasted ever so fine, or so I've heard. Although I've long since given up trying to tell if certain people from certain areas of the world tasted different.

The last time I really was a *young* woman was way back in the year 1475. I was twenty-one, to be specific. My full name was Anastasia Katarina Helena Romanov. But even at that age, I went by the nickname Tasia.

I'm originally from Odessa, Ukraine.

At the time, my country was being ravaged by the Great Plague. Entire villages were wiped out. Entire families. I'm afraid that's what happened with my family. I'm the only survivor. My parents and my two other sisters, Ekaterina and Suzana, were all taken by the Plague.

That's probably what left me so vulnerable.

I went to that tavern wanting to drown my sorrows. I had nobody left. Everyone that I knew in my village was gone, thanks to the Plague. So I came to the village tavern. That was probably my biggest mistake.

He was waiting for me.

Tall, with white-blond hair just like mine, the mysterious stranger had a way about him. He was a smooth talker. He was all too willing to buy me pint after pint of ale, along with hearty stew and warm bread.

Then he invited me up to his room at the inn next door.

I don't remember much after that. I'm not sure what happened. It was as if he'd put me under some kind of spell. When I woke the next morning, I had a strange set of bite marks on my neck, a nice pair of pink pinpricks that oozed slightly. The very next day, the bite marks were gone, as if they had never been there. Two days later, I tried to go out into broad daylight to find it burned my skin! Absolutely terrified, I ran back inside and instinctively knew not to go back outside until it was dark again.

When I did venture out, I found the darkness oddly comforting. It was as if it camouflaged or shielded me, somehow. And I found I had powers. I could hear things, like the beat of someone's heart, or their breath moving in their lungs.

That's when I started craving blood.

Family no longer mattered. Friends no longer mattered. Food or drink no longer mattered. Daylight no longer mattered. Finding victims to feed from was all that mattered.

That, and finding shelter before the sun rose.

He did that to me. To this day, I still didn't even know his name.

From then on, I wandered all over Europe, hoping to find him and tear him limb from limb for doing this to me. When international travel became possible, I took a steamship to America. Eventually I found myself at that city on the west coast.

I'm not sure what brought me back to Europe. Maybe it was a simple yearning to be back among what was familiar once again.

All I've found, however, are more victims to satisfy this lust, this craving for blood. The more I had, the more I wanted. Male victims were the easiest. One wink of these baby blues and I had men eating out of my hand. Until it was too late. My fellow females were the most difficult. When I wanted to hunt, to stalk, I'd go for a woman. But if all I wanted was blood, to feed, I'd find the first man to catch my fancy.

Fortunately, I didn't venture out much. Once I found a place to hole up in, I pretty much stayed there, until the need for blood brought me out once more.

The Germans could have conquered the entire European

continent for all I cared, until the ends of time, as long as it brought me more victims. I doubted British blood tasted any different. French, German, Russian or Italian blood, it all tasted the same to me.

But I was willing to see if maybe there was a difference, after all.

CHAPTER TWELVE: FROM THE PERSONAL JOURNAL OF AGENT LORENZO.

I had a pretty good idea what my first mission would be as an agent, although I arrived at that point in a roundabout fashion.

The first clue was when I took a class about London in the year 1940.

It was a grim time for the Allies in the Second World War. Germany was almost completely in control of Europe, except for Spain and Sweden, who had declared themselves neutral. England found itself the lone holdout.

The Americans wouldn't get involved until the next year, 1941.

German forces had run roughshod over the French army and air force. The British Expeditionary Forces had been driven to the French coast by the end of May. The Battle of Britain wouldn't truly begin until the first week of July, but in the meantime the evacuation at Dunkirk had been going on for about a week.

It would be a triumph for the British, a huge propaganda victory, and a black eye for the Germans, made possible by a fateful decision by one German general not to close in on the retreating British and French forces at the tiny village of Dunkirk.

By the end of the Dunkirk evacuation, more than three hundred thousand British and French soldiers were rescued, although they had to leave all their vehicles and a lot of their equipment behind.

The year 1940 would end, for the British, on a much better note, with the planned German invasion permanently postponed, although they would first have to endure the Blitz, the sustained night-time bombing raids courtesy of the Luftwaffe.

The second clue came with the class I took on British culture and mannerisms.

Once that class was done, Marie and I were both pulled in to a meeting with a senior agent.

That agent was none other than Andros.

As I entered the room, he said, "Agent Lorenzo. Good to see you again, my friend."

"Good to see you, too," I said, as if it had just been a few minutes since I had last seen him.

"I'm glad to see you completed primary training. But now your real work begins," he said, nodding to Marie as she came in behind me. "Have a seat, both of you. Let's get started."

We took our seats, exchanging looks as we did so, wondering why we both had been called in together. That question was soon answered.

"Well," Andros said. "The reason why you two are both here is simple. You are the only people who have encountered the vampire Tasia and lived to tell about it."

I said, "I'm guessing we think she's going to be in London?"

"Very good, Agent Lorenzo. Yes, according to the Annals, she was spotted in London during the Battle of Britain. Whenever a British city was about to be bombed by the Luftwaffe, she was there. People taking shelter in the subways made it easy for her to find new victims. The Blitz, especially, made it even easier. She just had to find a different subway tunnel.

"Your mission, however, won't be so easy. There is only one task. You are to locate Tasia, acquire her and kill her. By any means necessary. She has been quite good at evading our agents in the past, including myself, which is why I say you may use any means at your disposal in order to eliminate her."

So I asked, "How likely do you think it is that we'll be able to find her?"

"Good question, Lorenzo," he said. "If we're lucky, we might be able to question another vampire and get inside information."

"Ah," I said. "So that's our real mission? Intelligence?"

"Very good, Agent Lorenzo. Yes."

Marie asked, "Why can't we just backtrack to when she was first turned?"

Andros gave up a heavy sigh. "Trust me, we would, but we have been so far unable to determine the exact time and place when she was turned. So the best we can do is to make sure she never takes another human victim.

"But there is another reason, and that reason would be Rule Number One, which says we are only there to eliminate a given vampire or werewolf. We are not, repeat, not to change history in any way if we can avoid it."

"Rule Number One," I said. "Got it."

"I hope that you do," he said quietly. "Remember, you can be banished back to your own time period for breaking Rule Number One."

I silently swallowed at the import of those words.

Marie said, "Okay, we can't change history. How do we know that killing this vampire isn't going to change history?"

A look of surprise rapidly came and went on Andros' face. "Well, we do have some leeway," he said slowly. "However, there are other considerations."

"For example?" Marie prompted him.

"For example, we could go back to the exact moment in time when Tasia met the vampire that turned her. But we don't know for sure that preventing her from being turned then would have prevented her from being turned later. And then we wouldn't have you two. So there is that. Okay?"

It was Marie's turn to look surprised. "Uhm . . .okay. Wow. I hadn't thought of it that way."

Andros sighed. "I know that everyone has a moment in their lives they would just as soon had never happened. But how do we know, without that event, their lives would have been any better? So that's why we never change history. It could be you two are the only ones that can stop Tasia once and for all. But I have to brief you guys on a couple things before we drop you in to London."

"Okay," Marie said. "What else is there, sir?"

"In your case, Agent Marie, you might very well meet people in London that you used to know in San Diego. Fifteen years is not that long after the time we pulled you from. That's why we always drop an agent into a time period where they can't meet anyone they used to know. Even the possibility creates way too many potential complications. Remember, Rule Number One cannot be broken."

"Okay," Marie repeated herself. "So what do I do if I meet someone I used to know?"

"Preferably we would have you avoid them entirely," he replied. "If that's not possible, invent some cover story as to why you disappeared and why you're in London. Just make it plausible. I'm sure the war will help you there."

Marie fell silent. I'm sure she was probably thinking over all the *potential complications.*

Andros continued. "I'm not giving this lecture to Agent Lorenzo because he originally lived back in the Renaissance Period. The people who knew him have long since died."

I don't know why, but the weight of what he said hit me right at that moment. In fact, it hit me like a ton of bricks. But that was probably one of the reasons why I had been recruited, because I had no family left to miss me.

Marie patted my arm in a sympathetic manner.

"Your point being?" I asked, too quietly.

Andros coughed. "Only that you don't need to worry about meeting anyone you know in London at the time we're dropping you into. That's all I meant."

"Okay." I coughed too, getting back to business. "Anything else?"

"Yes," he said, grateful for the opening. "I'm going to be joining you, since this is your first case as Agents of Time."

"Awesome," I said.

Andros cracked a grin. "Yes, well, don't enjoy it too much," he said. "I'm not going to work the case for you, but I'll definitely be working the case with you."

"All right," I said. "When do we leave?"

"Not quite yet," Andros said. "We need to get you two outfitted for the mission. Namely, we need to get you into period clothes so you'll blend in."

"Okay," I said. "What else?"

"Then we'll take you over to Tech and have you briefed in on all the items you'll have at your disposal, including all the weapons you might need."

"Sweet," I said, but the reality was starting to sink in.

This wasn't training. As the saying went, now shit was getting real.

"As I said, let's get you two over to Tech," he said. "But before we do that, I wanted to speak with Agent Marie."

"About what?" she asked, sounding impatient.

"About what happens after we get Tasia," he said, sounding like he was trying to soften the blow.

"What do you mean?"

"The agent who recruited you told me you, to put it bluntly, are out for revenge."

Marie swallowed visibly. "Uhm . . .well, yeah. I want to get back at that bitch. She destroyed my life. I want to destroy her. She deserves no less."

"You can't go around with that kind of an attitude," Andros said, chastising her. "People with revenge on their minds tend to have a kind of tunnel vision. They get so focused on getting revenge that they, well, forget to live."

Marie sniffed. "I still miss my husband."

"After all this time," Andros observed.

"Yes," Marie said, sounding stubborn. "It feels like I left San Diego yesterday. I suppose I never really had time to grieve."

"I was afraid of something like that," he said, releasing another deep sigh.

Through the corner of my eye, I noticed him pull a device out of his pocket. I instantly recognized that device.

"Agent Lorenzo?"

"Yes?" I said.

"Could you please wait out in the hallway for us?"

"Uhm . . .okay." I was afraid to leave Marie by herself, but at the same time I also didn't want to have my memory modified, even by accident. "I'll just, uhm, wait out in the hallway."

"Thank you, Agent Lorenzo."

Chapter Thirteen: From the Personal diary of Agent Marie.

Once Lorenzo had closed the door behind him, silence settled down in the room.

I looked at him and said, "I hope you're not planning on modifying my memory."

I had never met Andros before. Being a senior agent, he was fittingly intimidating in appearance—tall, broad across the chest and shoulders, with a bald head. He could have a career playing offensive line in the NFL if he so chose.

But I knew, somehow, there was a pussycat under that gruff exterior.

Andros regarded me for a moment before replying, "And I hope you're not planning on going into the field with this desire for revenge." Holding up one hand to stop my reaction, he said, "Have you ever read the proverb that says having anger or revenge in your heart is like drinking poison and wishing the other person would die?"

"So what would you have me do?" I asked. "Forget about all that's happened to me?"

"Yes," Andros said. "At least, about what happened to you in the nightclub."

"May I ask why, sir?"

"You may ask why. What happened to you at that night club in San Diego happened. As much as we can or might want to, we can't go back and change it, not without risking changing history in some way."

"Why are you guys so keen on that?" I asked, the question suddenly crossing my mind.

Andros quietly replied, "Because, it appears as if it's your destiny to defeat Tasia. You and young Lorenzo."

That brought me up short.

In a thunderous flash of insight, the visions I'd had suddenly made sense. They were part of a story already told—and part of a story yet to be told. He was right. As much as I wanted to change what happened, by doing so, I would also change what happens next.

Shit. This time travel stuff sucked.

"All right," I finally said, after a moment of silence. "So you would have me, what, forget part of this even happened?"

"In order to accomplish the mission, yes," Andros said. "Listen, Marie, we have to stop this vampire. She's quite old, even for a vampire. We suspect she was first turned sometime about the year 1500 or so, but we can't be any more exact than that."

"Is she a primary or secondary vampire?" I asked, remembering the class.

"We don't know, not for sure, although we suspect she's just a secondary vampire. That makes little difference to her victims, though."

Silence fell in the room, during which I regarded the device in his hand.

"So. You would modify my memory? Just like that?" I snapped my fingers.

"If it meant getting the mission done, yes," Andros said. "Although there would be a side effect to it for you."

"What's that?"

"You would finally have some peace," he said quietly.

I wiped away sudden tears, with the realization that I haven't been able to fully commit to Lorenzo because I haven't been able to move past my husband's death. I would have thought that three years of training would have allowed me to do that.

But that hadn't been the case, or at least, that's what I told myself.

Just as Lauren had said, I'd suffered a traumatic event. It now appeared that it was one that I'd been unable to work through, or hadn't had a chance to work through.

"Would it work?" I asked. "Having my memory modified?"

"Yes," he said. "You wouldn't remember a thing. To the extent we would modify your memory."

"Okay," I said. "Do it."

"Are you sure?"

"No," I said. "But I also can't think of any other way to deal with this. And we literally don't have the time."

Andros smiled thinly. "Well, yes. You're right." He pointed the device at me. "All right, Agent Marie. In three. Two. One."

The room filled with white light—

—And when it faded out, I didn't feel any different, at least not that I could tell. So I tried to remember what was happening before.

I remembered being angry and sad, but I couldn't remember why. Just as I realized that, a most curious feeling came over me, like I was better off not knowing whatever it was I couldn't remember. *Oh, well . . .*

"Yes, Agent Marie?"

"Nothing," I said, standing. "I believe we were on our way to be outfitted for the mission."

"Yes," he said. "We were. Come on." And with one gentle hand on the small of my back, he ushered me from the room.

A little while later, the three of us were being outfitted for the mission. Specifically, I was being fitted for my wardrobe.

I had to blend in. Not only did I have to look like a lady, but as a lady would look in the 1940's, which was, in terms of fashion, vastly different from the Roaring Twenties. That meant no more drop waist dresses, which I was grateful for, or any of the short hairstyles.

After a lengthy wardrobe consultation, I stepped out in a standard forties' dress with a collar and buttons all up the front, with a trench coat over that, with a hat on, artfully tilted to one side. Then the stylist handed me a pair of stilettos. They were just like the Mary Janes I had worn in San Diego, except the heel was easily an inch or more higher, as well as thin, almost spiky. I shook my head, slipping them on.

As I stepped out, Lorenzo was giving me an odd look.

I said, "What?"

"Nothing. Just you look . . .great."

I laughed. "Thanks. I think."

However, Lorenzo wasn't looking too bad, himself, wearing a shirt and tie with an argyle sweater vest over it, along with nicely tailored trousers, and sneakers.

"How do I look?" he asked.

"Not too shabby," I said, looking him over, adjusting his tie and running my hands across his shoulders. "Pretty spiffy, in fact."

"Thanks," he said, cracking a grin that made my heart skip a beat.

"All right, you two," Andros said. "Come on, let's get over to Tech."

"Yes, sir," we both said.

Andros took us to yet another room, with two large tables in it, upon which rested a variety of objects, some of which I recognized as weapons, while others were disguised as ordinary objects. Andros directed me to one of the tables, on which were objects disguised as things a woman might carry in her purse. *Smart.*

Next to me, Andros picked up something I instantly recognized—a hand-held mirror, or what looked like one, anyway.

So I said, "I'm gonna go out on a limb and say this is not really a mirror."

Andros cracked a grin.

"No," Andros said. "Check it out."

So I looked at it closer. A street grid started to appear.

"That is a device that will hold a map of whatever city you find yourself in. And believe me, in a city like London, you are going to need it."

"Smart," I said. Then I picked up what looked like a set of keys. "I take it this is not a set of house keys."

Andros said, "Nope. That will return you here when your mission is done, by triggering a return effect in the time travel field. Once you trigger that, you can't go back, so I suggest you make sure you have your ducks in a row before you set it off, if you take my meaning."

"Meaning taken," I said. Then I picked up what looked like a tiny bottle of perfume. "I'm almost afraid to ask. But what's this?"

"That is holy water. If you find yourself in a situation with no good options, you can spray that at them and distract them while you make your getaway."

"Nice," I said. Then I picked up what looked like a flashlight. "And this?"

"That is your very own memory modifier," he said. "Use it very sparingly, or not at all. Usually we use it when there are witnesses. Just, if you do use it, take the time to invent a cover story for the person you use it on."

For some reason, that touched off a momentary reminder. But once again I had that feeling that it would be better to just forget about it. So I did.

Next to me, Lorenzo was looking over the objects on the other table. He looked like a child on Christmas morning.

Andros glanced his way. "If you have any questions, Agent Lorenzo, feel free to ask."

"Yeah," he said, picking up an object that looked like a metal flask for alcohol. "What is this supposed to be?"

"Be careful with that," Andros said. "That is truth potion, so try not to drink from it."

"Right," Lorenzo said, quickly screwing the cap back on.

"Besides, we won't need to use it, not with Agent Marie with us."

"What do you mean?" I said. Then I remembered. "Oh. Right."

"Yes," Andros said. "I've read in your file that you have a most unusual psychic ability."

"Yes," I replied. "Then you know it's a little . . .unreliable."

"I know," Andros said. "But it could definitely be useful."

I held my tongue. But I was filled with doubt and trepidation. I never knew what I would get when I touched someone. I also figured my unusual talent would be called into service.

That was just a matter of time.

I was going to have to learn how to work with it. More importantly, make friends with it.

Then Lorenzo picked up what looked like a bible. "I'm guessing this isn't a bible."

"Nope," Andros said. "Open it."

So Lorenzo flipped open the cover, to reveal two pistol clips.

"They're loaded with silver bullets," Andros said. "Just in case we meet any werewolves. I wouldn't put it past Tasia to have friends in London."

We both fell silent for a moment, considering the awful possibilities.

Lorenzo asked, "Has Tasia been spotted with werewolves

before?"

"No," Andros said. "But, as I said, I wouldn't put it past her."

"Hey," I said, having a sudden flash of inspiration. "That's what we are, in case anyone asks. Missionaries."

Andros nodded. "Good thinking. Hopefully nobody will ask. But that is good thinking. You have good instincts, Agent Marie."

"Thank you," I said, feeling my cheeks heat up.

Together we went over the rest of the objects. Then I took a large handbag and dropped each item inside it. I was being assigned a pistol, along with a fake bible with two clips inside, but no other weapons. And I was being assigned the ordinary objects.

"Okay," Andros said, breaking the expectant silence. "We're all set. Let's get over to the Portal and get this mission started."

Chapter Fourteen: From the Contact Report of Special Agent Andros.

Once the three of us had been appropriately outfitted and gotten the appropriate wardrobe for the period, we proceeded directly to the Portal.

Agents Marie and Lorenzo were subdued. I let them have their moment. I was the same way working my first case. More than likely it was hitting them finally that this was no longer a training exercise. This was, as they say, the real deal.

We entered an enormous room with extremely high ceilings and, at the other end, machinery, computer terminals, and several science specialists. The room was quiet, the sense of purpose palpable, nearly as palpable as the static electricity on the air, like a thunderstorm approaching.

The three of us headed across the room.

As we approached, the time travel apparatus came into clearer view. A ring sat on top of a circular pedestal, sunk in so that the inner edge of the ring was flush with the surface of the pedestal. The circle was large enough in diameter for me to easily step through without slouching or ducking down, while the pedestal itself was large enough to comfortably sit a house on.

I could feel my pulse quicken.

As we arrived at the other side of the room, one of the specialists stepped up to me. "Andros, good to see you, buddy."

I shook hands with him. "Good to see you, too, my friend,"

I said.

He looked past me. "New agents?"

"Yes," I said. "Agents Lorenzo and Marie."

He waved at them. "I'm Science Specialist Ming," he said. Ming was, like most Chinese men, tall, slender, and compact in build, except for a wild, unruly head of black hair.

"Hi," they said, waving in turn.

"First case, huh?" he asked, sounding sympathetic.

"Yes," I said.

"Let me guess," he said. "Second World War?"

"Right," I said. "Nineteen-forty, to be exact." I quickly described the time period and the location we needed to be dropped into.

"Okay, well, the Blitz didn't really start until September of 1940. So I'm dropping you in that time frame. Also, you're arriving in the late afternoon, almost dinner time. That'll give you a chance to establish yourselves and blend in before all hell starts breaking loose."

"Thanks," I said. "Ready, you two?"

"I think so," Marie said.

"Don't worry," I told her. "After this you'll be an old hand. It's just the first time you're going to be nervous."

Marie blushed as if she were being reminded of something more personal than just traveling through time.

As we spoke, the specialists bent to their tasks.

I watched as the ring began to spin. It spun slowly at first, but only a second later, it was spinning so fast that the markings on the metal blurred together.

A portal had appeared inside the ring. It looked as if it was just the view out of a window, except the view flickered every now and then.

"Time travel effect field is stable," Specialist Ming said, although he had to raise his voice in order to do so. "I suggest you three not dawdle."

"Come on," I told them.

"Good hunting," Ming said.

"Thanks," I told him.

Then the three of us stepped on to the pedestal.

The metal was noticeably warm, even through my boots. I took that moment to look back at my two charges. They looked understandably scared. In fact, Marie was holding Lorenzo's hand, clutching it like she would never let go.

Ah, young love.

Then I said, "Come on, you two. We have a mission. Let's get to it."

They seemed to snap out of whatever mood they were in.

"Yes," Lorenzo said. He glanced at Marie. "He's right. Let's move." Then he looked over at me, making a hand gesture. "After you. We're right behind you."

So I stepped through the Portal.

The transition from the Portal to London was seamless. I took a step through the Portal, and when my foot touched ground, I was in London. I had the brief sensation of stepping through what felt like static electricity, similar to stepping under a shower nozzle, through the water and back out again, but that was it.

I quickly took a few more steps, just in case someone happened to look up and see me. They wouldn't have seen anything unusual.

Then I looked back, to see Agent Lorenzo and Agent Marie had both come through.

Once I had made sure Lorenzo and Marie were both in one piece, I took a good look around to take stock of our situation.

Yes. London. Monday, September 16, 1940, to be exact, at a quarter till five in the afternoon, judging by the level of activity on the street and the sidewalk.

That would soon change.

I quickly glanced around. All around me were all the major London landmarks, including Buckingham Palace.

"So, this is London," Marie said, looking around with interest.

I smiled. "Enjoy it while you can," I said. "Sunset is in about an hour and a half. That's when the fun begins."

Marie's face changed. "I read that all the children were sent out of town to the country. That must have been upsetting for them."

"Yes, and they were sent for good reason," I said. "Come on, let's go find a pub or a coffee shop and start blending in."

Agent Marie took out the mirror that wasn't a mirror, flipped it open, and pretended to check herself out while she stared at it.

I cracked a grin. I couldn't help myself. I loved working with young agents.

All at once, Marie snapped the mirror shut. "There's a coffee shop just down that street. If we hurry, we can catch the afternoon tea rush."

"Let's go," I said.

A little bit later, we found a cozy little coffee shop right next to a bookstore. Marie was in absolute heaven, judging by the look on her face.

"Marie," I said, getting her attention.

"What?" she said.

"Remember, we are on a case."

She blushed. "Right. On a case." She seemed to compose herself. "Do you ever get to go a certain time period for like, you know, a vacation?"

"Sometimes," I said. "But agents who do that are always reminded of Rule Number One. Never change history."

"Right," she said glumly.

"Don't worry, I'll put in a good word for you."

"Thanks."

That seemed to brighten her day.

Just at that moment, the waitress came over. "All right, loves?"

"Good afternoon," I said.

"Americans, huh?" she said.

"Yes," Marie said. "Missionaries."

The waitress snorted. "You lot had better get back home to America and tell them to bloody well get their arses in gear."

"We'll get right to work on that," Marie replied. "But until then, we could use some tea and sandwiches."

"One platter for the three of you?"

"Yes, please."

"I'll be right back. Don't go anywhere, you lot."

"We wouldn't dream of it," Marie said.

"Well done," I said in a low voice, once the waitress had departed.

"Thank you," Marie said.

Service was fairly quick. The tea was excellent, even though I didn't really have a taste for it, wishing for a pint of ale instead, and the sandwiches were tasty.

I was just taking one last bite of my sandwich when Marie practically stamped on my foot.

That got my attention. "What was that for?"

Marie gestured with her chin.

I turned in my seat towards the entrance.

Bingo. Target acquired.

He'd just come inside. He was a little too pale, with short, unruly dark hair and bright, pale blue eyes. I got a bad feeling just looking at him.

"Little early for the creepy-crawlies to be coming out of the woodwork, isn't it?" Lorenzo asked from behind his teacup.

"Not necessarily," I said. "All the human traffic would draw them out. Plus, as you know so well, it's about ten minutes before sunset."

"More than likely he knows where Tasia is."

"I would guess so, as well," I said. "But not necessarily."

"I agree with Lorenzo," Marie said very quietly. "Let's tail him, at least."

I turned back to Marie. "Let's be on our way, shall we?"

She inclined her head in a single nod. "I'll get the waitress."

It took less than five minutes to get the waitress and settle the bill. Once that was done, I said, "What do you two think? Did he come up from underground, or somewhere nearby?"

Sometime during paying the check, our vampire had gone off somewhere. We had to locate him—fast.

"I say we track him down and find out firsthand," Marie said evenly.

I cracked a grin. This one was a tiger.

In the meantime, I was glad that Marie had submitted willingly to having her memory modified. Freeing her from her own memories was turning out to be the best thing I could have done for her.

But I didn't have time to pat myself on the back. I said to her, "Well, let's see if we can reacquire him, first. More than likely he's doing the same thing we are, blending in. He won't do anything to stand out, not if he's smart."

Quite all at once, the game changed.

Air raid sirens began singing their banshee wail. In true British stiff upper lip fashion, the people in the coffee shop didn't even turn pale. With an admirable degree of fatalism, they simply collected their things and rose from their tables, as if they had all the time in the world.

I turned to one young lady at the next table and said, "Excuse me, but where's the nearest underground station?"

She smiled. "Americans?"

"Yes," I said.

"Fortunately it's not too far away. Just down the street. You lot ready to go?"

I had to admire her calm attitude. Somewhere in the skies above the English Channel, dozens of bombers were climbing to altitude, their bomb bays loaded with incendiary bombs.

Their destination was here. London.

But I wouldn't have known it from this young lady's expression.

I said, "Yes, we are ready. If we could walk with you, that would be nice."

She winked. "I'm Ginny. Welcome to the neighborhood. Right this way."

"After you," I said.

Marie stood next to me, grinning a mile wide, and said, "You old smoothie."

"Thanks. Let's go."

"But what about our friend?" Lorenzo asked quietly.

"Just cool your heels," I said, even more quietly. "In case you haven't noticed, we have no choice but to head for shelter, otherwise we stand out. So we do what they're doing."

"Right," Lorenzo muttered.

"Cutting it a bit close, aren't we?" Marie said, looking around anxiously.

The sky was almost fully dark. Powerful klieg spotlights were shining their beams into the sky. The air raid sirens were getting louder. And I was pretty sure that, if I listened hard enough, I could just hear the approaching Luftwaffe bombers.

I tried not to think about it too much.

Meanwhile, civil defense workers were still ushering civilians into the Underground shelters. .

I turned to Marie and replied, "It can't be helped. But don't worry, they're working as fast as they can."

"They're actually moving pretty quickly," Ginny said,

looking at Marie. "Don't worry, love. We'll be safe and sound before the bombs fall."

"If you don't mind me asking, how can you be so blasé about this?"

The woman's face turned misty. "My brother. He was a fighter pilot with the RAF. He was shot down a couple of weeks ago."

Marie clapped her hand over her mouth. "Oh my god, I'm so sorry."

"It's down to me now to show a good example," Ginny said quietly.

The words were no more out of her mouth than the last people were let into the subway station. We all proceeded quickly but quietly down the steps.

The three of us spent an uneasy night in the subway station, pretending to sleep while trying our best not to. Even though the Luftwaffe bombers were gone in just a couple of hours, it took the whole night to sweep the city for unexploded bombs, put out the fires raging across the city, and take casualties to the hospital.

About an hour before sunrise, the air raid sirens began to issue the all-clear.

Just after that, we spotted our friend, headed up the steps, not wasting the hour he had to find shelter from the impending sunrise. And he was in a bloody hurry, as the British would say. As one person, Lorenzo, Marie and I all headed up the stairs to street level.

We came up the last step just in time to see our friend headed down the sidewalk, not even bothering to look over his shoulder. It was fortunate that he didn't seem to have any friends with him, as I would have expected.

"Agent Lorenzo?"

"Yes, sir?"

"Do you have your weapon ready?"

"Yes, sir."

"Good. You'll finally get to use it. Try not to miss."

"Right."

Doing so in a way that wouldn't attract attention, he eased the crossbow from his satchel, then reached in for a stainless steel, case-hardened crossbow bolt, fitted it to the string and nocked it back until it clicked in place.

I promised myself I wouldn't get mad if this plan didn't work.

There were one of three ways this could have turned out. First, Lorenzo could have just plain missed. I wouldn't have been happy, but that wouldn't have been the worst thing that could have happened. Second, he could hit the bullseye, piercing the vampire right through the heart and sending him back where he came from. That wasn't quite the outcome I had in mind, but I wouldn't be able to fault him for that, either.

We wanted to pump this vampire for information. For that to happen, Lorenzo had to hit the vampire so that it spit him through with the crossbow bolt without hitting anything vital.

It was a tricky shot. I didn't even trust myself to do it right.

So it was all on young Lorenzo to get the job done. Hopefully he was up to the task.

I couldn't believe our luck when we turned the corner and saw our vampire pause before entering an alley, looking one way and the other.

Lorenzo lifted the crossbow.

And squeezed the trigger.

The results were all I could have hoped for. The bolt pierced the vampire right through the midriff and *thunked* into the wood siding of the building next to him, holding him fast.

Lorenzo and I exchanged a quick grin. But that was all the celebrating we had time for. Just like for our friend, time was short. We quickly ran over to him, but kept a safe distance when we arrived, well out of range of its teeth and claws.

He was trying to pull the bolt out, but it had penetrated straight through his torso and into the wood. He wouldn't be pulling it out very quickly, not anytime soon.

"What have you done," he said, tugging at the bolt.

"Listen up, my friend," I said in a low voice. "We don't have a lot of time, and quite frankly, neither do you."

"Let me go," the vampire said urgently.

"Help us, and we'll help you," I said agreeably.

"What do you want?"

"The location of the vampire Tasia," I said. "We know she's in the area. Tell us where she is, and you might get underground before sunrise."

"Sorry, I don't know what you're talking about," the vampire said, his face and voice pinched with urgency.

"Fine," I said abruptly. "Sorry to do this, my friend." I gestured to Lorenzo. Quickly we got our friend in a joint lock, rendering him completely immobilized and helpless.

"Agent Marie," I said. "You're up."

"Right," she said.

Chapter Fifteen: From the Contact Report of Agent Marie.

The vampire was completely immobilized by the joint lock Andros and Lorenzo had him in. I didn't waste time. I lightly placed my fingers on any exposed skin I could see, careful to avoid the fangs and claws.

The street, the alley, everything disappeared. This time I was ready for it.

I was on the roof of a building. I didn't know which. I did know it was some time during the night. A bright three-quarters moon was visible through high cirrus clouds.

Nearby, the Eiffel Tower stood, gleaming dully in the moonlight.

On the roof with me were two other vampires. One of them was Tasia, looking beautiful for once in human form, pale skin, white-blonde hair and baby blue eyes. The other was unknown, name-wise. But in other ways, I knew him all too well. He was tall, male, with sleek white-blond hair and a definite air of malice and power about him.

Tasia was helpless before him. I'd made sure of that. I had her arms pinned behind her so she couldn't move.

Tasia's master was my master. I was required to do his bidding. I'm just glad I was on his good side.

"My dear, why do you go for female victims?" the male vampire asked quietly.

"The same reason you do," Tasia replied. "That's how you chose me, right?"

"I see you're enjoying Europe," the master vampire said.

"What can I say. The war has been good for me."

"I'm glad to hear that," he said. "But it's time to say goodbye."

"Why do you say that?"

"We're sending you to America," the master said.

"Already been there," Tasia said.

"Not where we're sending you," he said. "A small town in Pennsylvania. You'll be able to sleep in peace for decades."

Tasia struggled in my arms. "Why?"

"My dear, you've attracted attention to yourself. Your mission to London did not do you any favors. There is a price on your head."

"What does that have to do with me?" Tasia asked. "I can take care of myself."

"I disagree," the male vampire said coldly. "Get ready to be loaded in your coffin. Don't worry, we put in lots of padding."

He snapped his fingers in my direction. I knew what to do.

There was a door nearby that led to a stairwell. Tasia struggling every step of the way, the three of us made our way over to the door.

"You two are going to regret this," she said, struggling helplessly.

My master laughed, a quiet, malevolent laugh. "My dear, you are in no position to make threats. But it's nice to see you haven't changed, not since that night so long ago. Blood never tasted as sweet as your blood did."

"Speaking of which. Let me go and I'll tear you limb from limb for doing this to me," Tasia promised.

Master's eyes glittered. I knew from his expression he was tempted. "My dear, I did you a favor. As I recall, you had nobody left. No family. No friends."

A tear coursed down Tasia's face. "If you were looking to do me a favor," she said, her voice tight with memories, "you should have kept sucking till there was nothing left."

There was a long, stony silence. Then he said, "Some other time, I'm afraid, Tasia. Come on, let's get her down the stairs."

"Yes, Master," I said.

"Before we get busy with the loading," Master said quietly. "There's something you should know. If you are discovered, there is

another house out in the country you can retreat to in case it should become necessary."

Master held the door open. I proceeded through, guiding Tasia ahead of me.

Suddenly the alley was back. I had to lean on the nearest building. I had an afterimage in my mind's eye, like blinking after being blinded by a bright camera flash.

It was the house from my vision.

"Well, Agent Marie?" Andros asked. "Find out anything?"

"Yes," I said. "But I think it's a good idea for us to discuss it elsewhere."

"Yes, I would agree." They carefully let the vampire loose from the choke hold. "Well, my friend, we thank you for your time," Andros said.

"What about me?"

"What about you," Andros said coldly. "Enjoy the sunrise, won't you?"

"You said you'd let me go!"

"If you helped us," Andros replied. "And you didn't help us. We had to, ah, persuade you."

"Let me go," he said, still struggling. But every time he tried to free himself, it just made his situation worse.

"And let you take more human victims? I'd say the people of this city have suffered enough. Enjoy the afterlife, my friend."

Lorenzo and Andros stood next to me. I slipped an arm through each of theirs, the return device in my palm. Andros gave me a single nod.

I took the return device and activated it. London disappeared in a flash of white light.

Part Four: Nowhere to Run

Chapter Sixteen: From the Contact Report of Special Agent Andros.

Once we were safely back at headquarters, I took my two charges to the council to make our report.

"So, you think you have a lead on where Tasia might go next?"

"Yes, sir," I said. "A very good lead, as it turns out."

"Very good," said the Director. "It seems these two agents have proven themselves in the field. Nice work, you two."

"Thank you," they both said.

"No time to rest on your laurels, I'm afraid. You three get back to work. Resume your search for the vampire Tasia."

"Yes, sir," we all said, and left the council chamber.

From the council chambers, we headed straight to the library. I noticed Agent Lorenzo looking around.

"Penny for your thoughts, Agent Lorenzo?"

"Oh, I was just thinking how strange it feels to be here as an agent instead of as a cadet."

"You'll get used to it," I told him. "You'll have privileges as an agent you never had as a cadet. Come on."

In the central hallway, we paused.

"Agent Marie," I said. "The vampire told you Pennsylvania. Correct?"

"Yes," she said. "I'm afraid that leaves quite a lot of searching to do."

"Not as much as you might think," I assured her.

Just as I said that, one of the librarians, Erica, according to her nametag, came right up to us. "Hi, guys," she said to us. "How can I help you?"

"Property records," I said. "State of Pennsylvania, United States. The year 1940."

"Right this way," she said, turning at once, walking away.

Erica led us to the appropriate section of the library, set us up at a nearby computer terminal, then left us to our searching.

"Uhm, so what exactly are we searching for?" Marie asked.

"Houses," I said. "Ones that have been abandoned. Houses that have resisted attempts to own or renovate them."

"Ah," Marie said.

"Let's get to work," I said.

It took us exactly an hour.

Just as I thought this was going to take us a little longer than I first expected, Marie called us over to her terminal.

"Agent Andros?"

"Yes, Marie?"

"I think I've found it."

So I went over to her terminal.

"Check this out," she said.

She had a newspaper article blown up, showing an old house in Johnstown, Pennsylvania, about two hours east of Pittsburgh, where a work crew was taking a handsome old coffin down to the basement.

The article was dated December 1, 1940. That would fit.

"What else does it say?" I asked.

"Well, among other interesting details, it says the work crew was paid a lot of money to not ask any questions. And there's something else," Marie said, pausing significantly.

"And what would that be," I said, prompting her.

"I checked ahead," Marie said. "That house has been untouched since then. Until this date."

"Which is?"

"September 30, 2019," Marie said. "A homeless couple taking shelter in a terrible thunderstorm picked the wrong house to take shelter in. Neighbors heard screaming mixed with laughter and called the cops, who arrived to discover two people with no blood left in their bodies and an identical set of puncture marks on their necks."

"Yep, that's it," I said. "Still got your kits, kids?"

"Yes," they both said.

"Good. Let's get new wardrobe for that time period," I said.

"You really think we'll find Tasia," Lorenzo said dubiously.

"Agent Lorenzo," I said sharply. "Do you doubt Marie's detective work here?"

"Of course not," he said, just as sharply. "But what makes you think we'll be able to draw a vampire out of its slumber?"

I took a deep breath. That was a good question. I asked, "What do you think would bring a vampire as old as Tasia out of a decades-long slumber?"

"Fresh meat," Marie said, shuddering.

"Fresh blood," I said, seconding her. "Come on, you two. We don't have time to waste. And we're gonna need some help on this one."

"There's one more thing," Marie said, nervously biting her lower lip.

"What is it?" I asked, wondering what this could be.

"Just before I broke contact with our friend," she said, "I got a flash of an old house. The same old house I saw in a vision I got from Lorenzo."

"Really," I said. "And?"

"Well, I did some additional checking. Those two houses are listed as having the same owner. That can't be a coincidence."

"No, it can't be," I said. "As I said, come on, you two. We don't have time to waste."

"Still on the case, I see," Ming said, a little while later.

"Yes," I said. Then I told him the date, the location and especially the time we needed to be dropped into, preferably while it was still daylight.

"I'm on it," he said agreeably. "Sunset on the date in question is around seven or so. I'll drop you in around six-thirty."

"Sounds good," I said.

The science specialists bent to their tasks once more. I watched as the ring began to spin. Less than a second later the ring spun so fast the markings on it blurred together.

A moment later, a quiet suburban street could be seen inside the ring.

"Effect field is stable," Ming pronounced over the noise.

"Thank you," I said. "Come on, you two."

A moment later, I was standing on a quiet street corner. Behind me, I heard my two charges as they emerged from the portal.

I knew Marie had followed without looking. The girl had a fondness for high heels. In this case she had on high heeled patent-leather boots.

Once I had confirmed my two charges had arrived, I took stock of our surroundings. We were on a quiet, tree-lined, suburban avenue, with trees and houses in both directions.

Across the street on the opposite corner was a convenience store. Nearby, on our street corner, was a house, obviously lived in.

And next to that, down the block, was the house in question.

It was two stories tall, and just as obviously long since abandoned, the front door boarded over, as well as a couple of windows missing.

Even in broad daylight, the house had a brooding feeling.

"Is that it?" Marie asked in a hushed voice.

"Yes," I said. "That's it."

"Gives me the creeps," she said.

"No kidding," I said.

"So how are we doing this?" Marie asked. "Are we going to let that poor homeless couple be Tasia's latest victims all over again?"

"You know the rule, Agent Marie," I said quietly.

"Yes, I know the rule," she responded. "I also don't like letting people die when we know we can stop it."

I sighed. "Agent Marie, get down to the park," I ordered her. "This vampire won't be satisfied with just two victims. You know it and I know it."

Marie sighed. "Fine. I'll go to the park."

"Agent Marie," I said.

"Yes," she said, her voice softer.

"Be careful, would you?"

"Of course," she said.

And she started walking off down the street, streetlights playing off her patent-leather boots as she walked, her trench coat flapping around her thighs.

"Was that a good idea?" Lorenzo asked quietly.

"We need agents in place to track Tasia's movements," I told him. "Just in case."

Young Lorenzo didn't look too sure about that.

I said, "Agent Marie is capable. I trust her, and so should you."

"Yes, sir," he said dutifully. He looked at the house. "So. How much longer we got?"

"Not long," I said. "There's only about half an hour till sunset."

"Where's that help you mentioned?"

"They're already here," I said. "Don't worry about Agent

Marie. She's already being watched over. I have a team in place."

"Okay." He still sounded doubtful. "In the meantime, the weather is about to get rough."

I cast a wary eye to the sky. "Yes. Let's get under cover."

Chapter Seventeen: From the Personal Diary of the Vampire Tasia.

Date unknown
Somewhere in rural Pennsylvania

Without knowing why, I felt myself waking up. For a moment, I simply lay there, feeling the padding under my back, as well as the padding under my fingers and the wooden coffin lid directly over my head.

For a moment, memories replayed themselves in my mind.

Moonlit nights in Paris, completely ignoring the war. Having my pick of German officers and scared Parisian citizens. Then having my pick of brave English fighter pilots and the housewives who loved them, and blithely ignoring my orders.

Being unceremoniously stuffed into a coffin.

I wondered if that kind German doctor who fixed my cross burns was even still alive. Many times have I wondered what his blood would have tasted like.

Thunder.

I could hear thunder approaching. Far away, at first. But it was coming closer, growing louder, and coming fairly fast.

Blood.

I needed blood.

The need was subliminal, beyond conscious thought. It simply was.

Blood.

And then, quite distinctly, I heard noise, directly overhead.

Not even daring to move, I effortlessly tuned in with my senses.

Yes. A heartbeat. Two heartbeats.

Then I could pick out an abrupt click.

"Hah," said a male voice. "Got it."

"Honey . . ."

"What's your problem? We've been eighty-sixed from the homeless shelter. It is about to come pouring down rain and who knows what else. You wanna get caught in it?"

"No," said a female voice. "I also don't know if I want to go in there."

"It's an abandoned house," said the male voice. "What's the problem?"

"I've heard things about this house," said the female voice, in a hushed, fearful whisper.

From almost directly overhead there came a huge *clap* of thunder, making the whole house rattle. A moment later, rain began to fall. I could feel the rain pounding the frame of the old house in torrential sheets.

"See, now it's raining," said the male voice. "You coming inside or what?"

A moment of silence was the only reply.

"Listen, we'll only stay here a couple of hours. We'll let the rain pass and then we can be on our way. Okay?"

"Okay . . ."

Then I heard the unmistakable sound of a door being opened, followed by a door being closed. I could not believe my luck!

Two victims were literally walking into my arms.

Moving swiftly and silently as only a vampire could, I eased open the lid of the coffin and lifted myself to a sitting position. Then I lightly leaped over the side, landing on my

feet, and made my way over to the stairs.
    Dinner was about to be . . .served.

CHAPTER EIGHTEEN: FROM THE CONTACT REPORT OF AGENT LORENZO.

"Hey, what the hell —"

Ffft. Ffft.

Agent Andros shot both of the homeless people with a tranquilizer dart. Each crumpled to the floor with hardly a rustle.

"Nice shot," I said to him.

He cracked a grin. "Thanks. Just don't tell Agent Marie."

"Promise," I said.

We both spoke in barely audible whispers.

"Get ready," Andros said. "You're only gonna have one shot at this."

"Right," I said, taking a wooden crossbow bolt this time, fitting it to the string and sliding it back along the groove until it clicked into place.

I hefted the weapon without a word, indicating I was ready.

Andros gave a single nod.

Outside, rain was still falling, although it had started slackening. The lightning was also moving off, taking the frame-rattling crashes of thunder along with it.

I knew the team that Andros had called in was ready and waiting.

I could feel something coming up the stairs from the basement.

Everything went very still.

Everything went very quiet.

A shock of adrenaline pumped through me as I saw a pair of red eyes appear at the top of the stairs. And hold.

Come on, you bitch.

Wait for it . . . Wait for it . . .

I fired. My timing was damn near perfect.

"Aaaahhh!"

Damn. I didn't miss, but I didn't get the sweet spot. The heart of the matter, one could say.

A heartbeat later, a shape came at me. I didn't even think this time. Without a moment to lose, I lifted my cross in its way.

"*Aaahhhh!*"

With a crash of broken, splintered wood and shattered glass, Tasia left the house like a bat out of hell, headed in a random direction.

"Shit," I said, heart pounding at my close call.

"Are you all right?" Andros asked, sounding concerned.

"Am I?" I asked in return.

"Let's see," he said, lifting my chin.

"If I'm not, end me," I said.

"No," he said. "She didn't get you." He let go of my chin. "Damn, kid, you are getting good with that cross."

"Thanks," I said. "What do we do now? It shouldn't be too hard to track a vampire with an arrow in her and a fresh cross burn."

"You might be surprised," Andros said. "But let's get the word out. Hopefully Marie can spot her for us."

I just stared at the floor. *Let her be safe.*

"I'm sure Agent Marie will be just fine."

I saw his grin. "Thanks."

He clapped me across the bicep.

"Andros to Marie. Heads up. You got company incoming. And she's injured."

"Copy, Andros. We're on it."

Chapter Nineteen: From the Contact report of Agent Marie.

One of the many good things about this time period was that people carried personal communication devices everywhere they went. So we didn't stand out in any particular way by talking into a tiny device.

The thunderstorm had begun to move off. Flashes of lightning lit the sky in the distance, and those big claps of thunder no longer shook me to my bones.

Moving quickly, we took up our stations in the park. There was still a stiff breeze, blowing flecks of rain off the trees.

Otherwise, all was deathly still.

No birds were singing. Nothing was moving.

Despite myself, I was a little afraid. How does a vampire behave when it's up against a wall, with nowhere to run or hide, having been flushed out of hiding?

"In position, Agent Marie," a voice whispered in my ear.

I waved to nobody in particular. From a nearby rooftop, a sniper waved in return. I knew he had a rifle nearly as long as he was tall, semi-automatic, with a scope and a silencer, with orders to shoot first and not ask questions at all.

I was playing bait. Pretty bait.

To that end I wore a khaki trench coat over a cotton dress and black patent-leather boots, a large suede handbag slung over my shoulder. I even had my hair up in a bun.

I was sitting on a park bench like I had nothing better to do.

In my purse, I had several different weapons, including a pistol, loaded with silver bullets. They wouldn't do squat against a vampire, but the crossbow would. And of course I wore my gold cross.

No werewolves were in the vicinity. Fortunately there wasn't a full moon. That was about the only good thing in this whole situation. At least I wouldn't get eaten by a werewolf tonight.

I tried to relax. I was surrounded by layers of defense.

Would all those layers be enough?

Thinking I was going to need it, I quickly located the perfume bottle that wasn't and made sure it was charged up.

Then I rose from my park bench and made my way to the interior of the park, so the sniper would be able to cover me a little better.

Far away, lightning lit up the clouds.

A faint breeze came and went.

There was a crackle of static in my ear. "Agent Marie. I got movement. Three o'clock from your position."

I tried to simply let the moment come. I was bait, for one reason—make the vampire so injured she would have no choice to reveal her hideout, even though we already knew where it was.

There was movement in the corner of my eye.

A heartbeat later, I shifted into my feline form, and good thing, because a moment later, a set of teeth and claws came slashing through the air, just as I rolled over to get out the way. Tasia, in full vampire mode, completely missed and slammed into a nearby tree.

Just as quickly, the sniper took his shot.

"Aaaahhhh!"

Clearly injured, the wind knocked right out of her, she staggered off in a random direction, then whirled on the spot and vanished.

114

I cracked a grin, despite myself. The plan had worked.

I quickly resumed my human form.

The sniper said, "Agent Marie, report! Are you all right?"

"Yes," I said out loud. "I think you got her."

All around me, the park was coming to life. Birds were singing again. Crickets chirping.

"Agent Marie to Agent Andros. Do you copy?"

"Loud and clear, Agent Marie. Go ahead."

"I think we got her. What now?"

"Good job. Let's get back to headquarters."

PART FIVE: ENDGAME

Chapter Twenty: From the Contact Report of Special Agent Andros.

Once we got back to headquarters, the first thing I did was pull up the blueprints for the house in question.

Yes, it was the ideal location for a vampire to take shelter in—isolated, easy to defend and difficult to find.

Unless you knew what to look for. And we did.

"All right," I said. "According to the tracking device contained in the round we put in Tasia, she is holed up at this house, the location for which we have, thanks to Agent Marie."

I tapped the holographic map. Marie blushed.

"The question becomes," Lorenzo said, "how do we get her to come out to play? I doubt she's going to fall for the same lure twice."

"You might be surprised, Agent Lorenzo," I said. "Vampires have pride. And unless I miss my guess, Tasia almost surely recognized you. Vampires have long memories, after all."

"So you think I might be able to hold her interest?" he asked.

"I know you will," I said. "At least, until we can bring some help."

"Yeah? Like what, sir?"

"Demolition equipment," I said bluntly. "If she won't come out to play, we'll go digging for her. One way or another, she will meet her maker."

"Yes, sir," he said. "We'll have another team in place?"

"Yes, we will," I said. "I suggest you get outfitted. Get loaded for bear."

"Yes, sir," Lorenzo said.

"That goes for you, too, Agent Marie," I said.

"Yes, sir," she said, sounding surprised.

"Get going, both of you. I'll meet you at the Portal."

"Yes, sir," they both said, heading for the Tech room.

This time, we've got you, Tasia.

Chapter Twenty-one: From the Contact Report of Agent Lorenzo.

M arie and I went straight to the Tech room to get outfitted. With a mental swallow I noticed there was less tech
and more weapons on the table.

With a casual ease born of much practice, Marie took a
semi-automatic rifle and selected from a range of accessories,
including a scope sight, silencer, and no less than three mag-
azines.

"Let me guess," I said. "Silver bullets, right?"

She winked. "Let's not waste time," she said. "Come on,
get moving."

"And I'm moving . . ."

Going through my own mental checklist, I selected a crossbow with a quiver of wooden and metallic arrows, two short
swords, and throwing knives. I wasn't sure if I would be able
to use the knives and get away, but if push came to shove, I
could shove back.

Stripping down to my waist, I put on a padded vest, then
a set of chain mail. Then I put on a waistcoat on over it, along
with a harness for the sheaths.

Decisively, I sheathed my swords. I was ready.

"Lorenzo."

I turned to face Marie. "Yes?"

"Don't you dare get yourself hurt," she said. "I've gone
through too damn much to lose you now. Copy that?"

"I copy that," I said. "So. You like me, huh?"

She winked again. "Don't tell Andros. More than likely they won't like that."

I cracked a grin, in spite of the solemn moment. "Nope."

She leaned in and kissed me. "Be careful."

"I will," I said.

Without another word, I headed to the Portal.

The people at the Portal were ready for me when I arrived. Word must have gone ahead of me. As I entered the room, the ring was already spinning madly.

And through the ring, an old house was visible.

"Time travel effect field is stable," said the lead science specialist, a woman this time, wearing glasses, her hair in a proper bun.

"Thank you," I said.

"Good hunting, Agent Lorenzo," she said. "And good luck."

With another mental swallow, I climbed on the pedestal. As soon as I did, I could feel a powerful vibration under my feet. The very air crackled with static electricity. Feeling every step, I approached the spinning ring.

I stepped through the Portal.

They say circles have no beginning or end.

So here I was. Out in the middle of nowhere. Except for the house, trees and grass were all there was, for as far as I could see.

Behind me, the sun was setting. Ahead of me, the moon was rising.

With a jolt of adrenaline, I realized why this night felt so familiar — this was the night from Marie's vision.

Shit.

Mist swirled around my legs as I slowly approached the wrought iron gate. For some reason my legs felt very heavy, my steps slow.

I had no choice but to enter this creepy old house. Or did I?

Just as I put my hand on the gate, a female voice said, "Hey, not so fast."

I turned. It was Marie.

"Hey," she said, a long rifle slung over her shoulder. "Decided to wait, I see."

"Well, yeah," I said. "I'm not stupid."

"I'm glad you did," she said softly. "Speaking of which—duck."

I didn't have time to argue. I hit the dirt.

She rapidly unslung the rifle, took aim at something unseen, and fired. *Spit. Spit.*

There followed the unique sound of an animal in pain.

Shit. There was a werewolf. Well, was. Now it was dead.

"I hope you have lots of ammunition," I said, picking myself up off the hard ground. "You might need it."

"I brought some," she said modestly. "You're welcome."

"Yeah, thanks," I said, brushing off my trousers.

"I hope you realized what night this is."

"Yeah," I said. "From your vision."

"Yes," she said quietly. "I never thought we'd actually get here."

"Yeah, seriously," I said. "So, what now? Do we sit here and let the rest of what's in there come out to play?"

"That's the plan," she said. "Unless you *want* to go in there."

I swallowed. "Not really," I confessed.

"I'm glad to hear that," Marie cracked. "What were you going to do with Tasia?"

"I'm going to make her walk right out into the brand-new dawn," I said flippantly.

"Uh-huh," Marie said dubiously.

"Seriously," I said. "That vision you got off our friend in London gave me an idea."

"Okay," she said. "Well, Special Agent Andros should be arriving any second now with some, uh, specialized equipment."

"Yeah?" I said. "Like what?"

"Explosives," she said bluntly.

"Cool," I said. "This should be a real blast."

Marie rolled her eyes, shaking her head. "Lorenzo . . ."

"Thanks," I said, cracking a grin.

Marie blushed.

Just at that moment, Andros himself materialized out of thin air, several people appearing along with him.

"Oh, good," he said. "Still in one piece, I see."

"So far, yes," I said. "We got a long night ahead and full clips locked and loaded."

"Very good," he said, inclining his head slightly. "You two keep watch. My team and I will get to work with these."

"Yes, sir," we said.

Chapter Twenty-two: From the Personal Diary of the Vampire Tasia.

Date unknown
Somewhere in rural Pennsylvania

How did they know? That was the only question flying through my stunned mind.

How did they know where to find me?

Master said the house was secure, that nobody would know about it. But someone was waiting for me at the house.

No, not just someone. That boy from the church in Italy, who gave me the painful burn scar that I wouldn't soon forget.

And he shot me, the little mortal. Not only that, but gave me another cross burn to boot. I was rattled, to my core. Another half an inch to the left and I wouldn't have been writing this.

If that weren't bad enough, that bitch from the nightclub somehow knew how to shift into an animal form, to match my reflexes with her own.

Mortals with decent weapons, and skills to match. This was not good. They could kill me.

And then I would finally get to see my family again . . .

Yes, I admit, I miss them. Long, lonely nights spent looking for the next victim were no match for sunny days, however lonely.

I was evenly split between wanting to kill them all, and simply wanting to end this.

The humans were skilled. And apparently they were looking for me. Unfortunately it was only a matter of time. I was wounded, badly. An arrow to the chest is a wound a vampire doesn't walk away from, regardless of where it hits.

Yes. The next time I met them in battle, I would gladly end this.

Chapter Twenty-three: From the Contact report of Agent Lorenzo.

Marie grabbed my arm and pointed. "Lorenzo, look." Dawn.

Yes, the sky off to the east was beginning to turn pearly pre-dawn gray. It had been a long night of waiting, punctuated by brief bursts of activity.

Now it was time.

Andros signaled to someone. With a crash, the driver of an earthmoving vehicle sent the scoop straight through the wall, crumbling it in seconds.

Exposing the basement.

Inside the basement was a coffin. Yeah, I know, so cliché. As if by itself, the coffin lid slowly began to rise, as though an invisible hand pulled the lid up along a hinge.

A voice spoke, echoing in the trees and settling down over the land.

"Who disturbs me in my rest?"

"I do," I said. "It's time for you to answer for all the blood you've shed, all the victims you've taken, Tasia."

Tasia popped out of the coffin.

I couldn't help but cringe. The arrow I'd fired was still in her. And the cross burn I'd given her was prominently visible. She was in vampire mode, eyes red, hair puffy, fangs extended.

Silently, I swallowed.

"You," she said.

"Yep," I said casually. "Me." I went to casually draw my swords, then stopped. "You know, your family misses you."

"What?"

"Your family," I repeated myself. "How did they die?"

The moment seemed to hang in the air. Then, right before my eyes, Tasia changed to human form. Just as I thought, she was beautiful, with pale skin, white-blonde hair and baby blue eyes. And so young.

"The plague," she whispered. "They were killed by the Great Plague."

"I'm sorry," I said. "The same thing happened to my family, too. My dad's whole family died of the plague."

Tasia said nothing.

"How did you become like this?"

Still no reply. Shit. I had to get her talking. Sunrise wasn't for another ten minutes, judging by the sky, which was steadily lightening.

So I tried another tack. "Doesn't this get tiring?" I asked.

Tasia rolled her eyes. "You have no idea," she said, her voice heavy with sarcasm.

"Wouldn't it be nice to just . . .give it all up? To just walk out to meet the sunrise?"

"Oh, god, it would be," she said.

I risked a glance off to the east. Sure enough, the sun was just starting to peek over the hills. So I eased over to the door in the one standing wall, that just happened to face to the east.

"Shall I get the door for you?"

"Yes, thank you," she said quietly.

I pulled the door open.

The vampire Tasia was blasted with the pure morning sunshine of a new day.

It didn't seem to be giving her any pain. If anything, she simply stood there, not fighting it, letting the flames consume her.

It was over in seconds.
Tasia was gone.

CHAPTER TWENTY-FOUR: FROM THE FINAL REPORT OF SPECIAL AGENT ANDROS.

"And so, Director, the Vampire Tasia has finally been eliminated."

"Excellent," he said. "And what do we know, if anything, about her followers?"

"At this point, I'm not certain she created any new vampires," I replied. "I think she was most interested in blood."

"All right. And what about your two charges? Lorenzo and Marie?"

"Director, I'd say they'd earned a vacation, if nothing else."

"Agreed," said the director. "Let me just extend my congratulations on a job well done."

"Thank you, sir," I said, as humbly as possible.

"Take some vacation time for yourself," the Director said. "And once you get back, we'll have a new case for you."

"What is it, sir?"

"Not now," he said. "Take some well-deserved time off. Dismissed."

"Thank you, sir."

And with that, I swept from the council chambers, in search of a pint of cold ale and a sandwich. I'd earned it.

The End
For Now

Julianna Lee sat at her favorite spot in her favorite coffee shop, sipping from her smoothie, slowly waking up, even though it was well past eleven in the morning.

She hoped Zach wasn't late as she checked the time on her cell phone. She didn't have a lot of time before she had to go to the yoga studio to meet with Hope and Robin.

She had some news for him. And he, according to his text message, wanted to ask her something. Her pussy had twinged when she saw the message.

Just a few days earlier at work, Roger Talbot himself had pulled her aside. "Miss Lee, may I have a quick word with you, please?"

"Of course, Mr. Talbot," she had said. After all, when the CEO said he needed to talk, what was she going to say — no?

"Miss Lee, it's Roger."

"All right," Julianna said. "Only if you call me Julie."

He smiled. "All right, Julie. I just wanted to let you know, in person, that I feel you've done such a great job filling in as the evening anchor that we'd like to make it official, and name you the new evening and late-night anchor."

Julie clapped her hand over her mouth. "Oh my god."

Roger's smile widened slightly. "Yes. I'm sure you know by now that Linda O'Neill has decided not to come back from maternity leave."

"Yes, I've heard."

"It took us by surprise, I can tell you. But as I said, you've done such a great job filling in for Linda that we would like to give you her anchor spot. What do you say?"

"I would love to!"

"Good. We'll have Hope announce it on tonight's prime time broadcast. Congratulations, Julie. You deserve it."

"Thank you," Julie said.

And with that, he walked away.

Julie was left in a daze as she stood there. Anchor!

Hope came right up to her and flung her arms around her. "Congratulations, Julie."

"Thank you," Julie said, her face beaming.

"Come on, let's get over to Wardrobe. We need to get ready."

"Right."

They proceeded directly over to Wardrobe. Christmas was coming up later that week. Hardly anyone was around, including the usual prime time anchor people.

As they entered the Wardrobe room, the attendant said, "What are you ladies feeling like this evening? I just got a bunch of new stuff."

Hope selected a very appropriate dress — white with diagonal red stripes — making her look like a candy cane. But Julie didn't say that out loud, especially when Hope emerged from the changing stall. She had to admit the dress went perfectly with the black patent-leather boots Hope had brought with her.

Julie, meanwhile, went for a more polished look, choosing a red satin blouse to go with a black leather pencil skirt that had a high waist and stopped right at the knees, finishing it with a pair of patent-leather open-toed heels.

And no bra.

When she did her evening segment on the prime time edition where she had to stand up, she had a feeling nobody would be changing the channel—that, and during the late-night broadcast, when people would be able to see her legs under the anchor desk.

"How do I look?" Hope asked as she closed the stall door.

"Very pretty," Julie said.

"Thank you. I still can't believe you had your boobs done," Hope said, pointing with her chin to Julie's obviously larger chest, the curve and swell of her cleavage peeking out from under her blouse.

"Why? You're the one who said I would benefit from bigger boobs."

"And my husband did an excellent job," Robin Meyers said as she entered the room, heading to the attendant's desk.

"Thank you," Julie said.

"I told you he was the best," Robin said, then ducked into a changing stall.

Julie had been on the fence for a long time about having her boobs done. Everyone had an opinion, either for or against. What had clinched her decision was the night she had tried the inserts the nurse had given her, to get her used to the idea of having larger boobs. That night the station's ratings went sky-high from just the hint she might be getting bigger boobs.

The procedure had gone perfectly, with no complications. Robin and Hope both had been with her at the clinic and had given her a ride home once the staff had cleared her.

The people at the station hadn't said as much, at least not out loud or to her face, but Julie was pretty sure she got the anchor spot because of her new boobs. And she wasn't about to start asking questions. Once the swelling had gone down and the incisions had healed, she'd started showing off her new boobs in public by wearing revealing tops, started noticing more glances from both men and women, and began to receive compliments.

While Robin was busy changing, Julie glanced at Hope. "Would you like to touch them?"

Hope hesitated. "Uhm . . .what?"

"Come on. I'm not having this attitude from you. It was your idea, but now it's like you're a whole different person."

Julie took a single step closer to Hope, whose hands were shaking as she raised them. No doubt she was remembering everything about her breasts that day in the shower and was wondering if they felt any different now.

Only one way to find out. Come on . . .

Finally, Hope rested her hands on Julie's breasts, exhaling out loud, as if in pleasure.

"They feel good, don't they?"

Hope nodded but didn't speak, swallowing visibly.

All at once Robin emerged from her stall, wearing a brown satin blouse, white pencil skirt, and matching white heels.

Julie noticed that Hope did not take her hands away.

Cocking an eyebrow, Robin said, "If you're finished touching Julie's new boobs, we need to head over to hair and makeup."

The three of them laughed, Hope's attitude disarmed, the spell broken. Hope took her hands away, although she did it slowly.

ABOUT THE AUTHOR

Jon Bradbury has been published by eXtasy Books since 2004, including *Colorblind*, *Midnight Blue*, *We'll Always Have Paris* and *Sugar Daddy*, just to name a few. When he's not writing or editing, Jon can be found reading, listening to music, watching movies on TV, and surfing the net. Jon is currently single and resides in Johnstown, PA.

Jon invites you to visit his website for more information: http://bradburyjon.wix.com/jonbradburynovelist